BEACHMASTER

Bird's
Neck Is.

Region
of
Ice

Come, lions that dwell in the sea,
We travel far in mystery

Small Crab
Is.

Heat
Vent

The
Cove

Is. of
Bones

The
Sargasso

Laboratory

Tom Shachtman

BEACHMASTER

A Story of Daniel au Fond

Illustrated by
Jamichael Henterly

HENRY HOLT AND COMPANY • NEW YORK

Published in the United States by
Henry Holt and Company, Inc., 115 West 18th Street,
New York, New York 10011.
Published in Canada by Fitzhenry & Whiteside Limited,
195 Allstate Parkway, Markham, Ontario L3R 4T8.

Library of Congress Cataloging-in-Publication Data
Shachtman, Tom, 1942–
Beachmaster : a story of Daniel au Fond / by Tom
Shachtman ; illustrated by Jamichael Henterly.
—1st American ed.
    p. cm.
Summary: An account of the adventures of a sea lion,
including his experiences with man in a sea laboratory and his
assumption of the role of beachmaster or head of the tribe.
ISBN 0-8050-0498-X
[1. Sea lions—Fiction.] I. Henterly, Jamichael, ill.
II. Title.
PZ7.S526Be 1988
[Fic]—dc19   88-13391
                                          CIP
                                          AC

Henry Holt books are available at special discounts
for bulk purchases for sales promotions, premiums,
fund raising, or educational use. Special editions
or book excerpts can also be created to specification.

    For details, contact:

    Special Sales Director
    Henry Holt & Co., Inc.
    115 West 18th Street
    New York, New York 10011

First American Edition

Designer: Victoria Hartman
Printed in the United States of America
10 9 8 7 6 5 4 3 2 1

for my son
Daniel Shelare Shachtman

CONTENTS

Part One—Alone

1. The Cove 3
2. The Legend 15
3. Leaving 26
4. Alone 36
5. Strange Grazing 43

Part Two—Being Tested

6. The Laboratory 57
7. The Floater 65
8. Escape 73
9. Sargasso 77
10. Home Again 90
11. The New Beginning 98

Part Three—Together

12. Together 109
13. Cousins 114
14. Nightmare 122
15. The Task 129
16. The Last Attack 137
17. The Tribe 148

Part One

ALONE

1 · THE COVE

*O*ut beyond the cove's encircling walls the sea was restless and cool, but within, it was warm and calm. At leap tide the gentle waves hardly broke foam as they rolled in to the worn cliffs. As the sun emerged in white heat from the mountain that loomed to the east, the mists of dawn disappeared.

Hagis and Achitopel, two young bulls, were amused by a brown, dried-kelp thing with biped food in it that had lodged near Goshun's sleeping perch. Thrown down by the previous evening's watchers, it evidently had not disturbed the old Whistler. The bulls made a game, each jumping up alternately until Hagis succeeded in knocking the kelp thing off the perch. Then they ate the biped food, tore the dried-kelp thing to shreds, and let loose on the currents the metal worm that had been inside.

Just beneath the surface, two older cows, Blossom and Esther, sportchased the biped metal worm as if it were a stray fish that had wandered into the cove. When it did not swim away, they lost interest. The metal worm drifted downward. Its progress was noted by Daniel au Fond, birth brother of Hagis and Achitopel, who sat, as his name had it, on the bottom.

Daniel had been awake for some time, making his rounds of the cove's nether limits, investigating what the night had stirred into the tribe's home. The skin of the metal worm was smooth and tasteless; not even a barnacle would grow on it. Daniel left it for the bipeds, who would come and remove all their objects from the bottom in a day or two.

Daniel found and grasped in his foreflippers an abalone shell of irregular size and brilliance. He carried it first to the surface, then up on the rocks several levels to Bright Corner, a niche at the edge of the southernmost tide pool. Because he was not yet full grown, Daniel could reach Bright Corner only at leap or long tides, not at low or lull, and it was always a struggle to clamber up to the top level. Flipper holds in the vicinity of the Singing Stones were few and tricky. Younger sea lions weren't supposed to go anywhere near this area; Daniel ignored the warning, but it served to keep others out. The warning and the difficult climb gave to Bright Corner the privacy he needed to do his work.

Once atop the ledge he propped the abalone shell at a vertical angle, using a piece of fir driftwood. It occurred to him that the driftwood's edge ought to echo the egglike curve of the new shell. He sat with the wood between his foreflippers and gnawed it into shape. Later, the declining sun would be reflected by the shell onto other objects—rounded sandstones, a trilobite in amber, the saw of a cuttlefish. He imagined the sun bathing them all with colors that would alter moment by moment as the evening approached. It didn't matter if the tribe thought this was silly. He was making something to honor the dying sun, during the Singing, and that was that.

"Daniel! Daniel Digger, come down and race."

It was Hagis, the jokester of the birth cohort, but even the taunt, that hated nickname, didn't budge Daniel from the driftwood. Hagis circled and leaped up several times to look at Daniel, but he hadn't perfected the trick of reaching the ledge and, each time, fell back into the water.

"You keep eating that wood, you'll get splinters in your brain," Hagis warned. When that didn't move Daniel, he said, "Tashkent'll bash you for being up there."

"I'll race with you later." Daniel phrased his no carefully. Actually, he'd stopped enjoying the endless contests and preferred to sit and gnaw a piece of wood, to make a treasure to honor the evening sea's swallowing of the sun— but he didn't want to say so, not even to Hagis, for fear of being considered ill or strange.

Hagis swam off. Daniel settled back down on the high ledge. From atop Bright Corner he could compare the waters inside the cove and outside in the endless ocean. Why were the far waters so blue? Why didn't the waves out there behave in the same way as those that entered the cove? What were those floaters with bipeds on them? When he was younger he'd asked such questions of the tribe's beachmaster, Tashkent—but the huge, dominant bull had just brushed Daniel aside with the warning that he should mind what was happening inside the cove, not outside.

Down below, the bulls sprinted between northern and southern arms of the cove. They stayed clear of Tashkent the Terrible, but also made sure to have their fun in full view of the cows. Displaying their trim, muscled bodies, Hagis, Achitopel, and other adolescent males dashed toward one wall or the other at breakneck speed, and only at the last moment flipped over into somersaults to make the hard turns. Young and older females lay on the low perches, grooming themselves with foreflippers, watching the show-offs. Anna, the most beautiful of the adolescent females, dove gracefully into the waters, wet herself thoroughly, transforming her fur into a bright, brown sheen that would dry to a golden tan. Then she clambered up to air herself. As she did so, every male eye in the cove turned to watch—including Daniel's.

He would have to apologize to Anna for leaving her last night at moonrise after their tryst in Grunting Cave. But the rockfish that had come into the cove by mistake had to be investigated, chased, outmaneuvered, and eaten. It was alive, not dead and dull like the food the bipeds threw in every evening. He'd asked her to hunt with him, but she'd refused. She'd told him that she, too, dreamed of the ocean outside the cove—why, then, wouldn't she join in hunting one of its creatures? Daniel thought that he'd never understand females, but promised himself he'd apologize to Anna. She really was very beautiful, and she was the only cow who shared some of his dreams.

"Aaaarrghhh!"

The groan was followed by a crash into the waters, then by the bark of laughter from the racing bulls. Gazing down, Daniel saw old Goshun lying half-submerged near the moss-covered slope below Whistler's Shelf, and guessed that the old white-fur had slipped while asleep and had hit the water, flat and harsh on his belly. The big bull was so blubbery that he seemed helpless in the water. Daniel moved down to investigate.

As Daniel cautiously swam near, Goshun growled and showed the teeth that, tribal stories told, had kept him invincible until that distant day when Tashkent had taken over the dominance of the tribe and relegated Goshun to the position of lead singer. Daniel was surprised to note that the once-feared teeth had all but rotted away; he wondered if others knew of this infirmity. Goshun grappled his way onto the slippery moss, then turned so that his back nestled in the cliff and he faced the water—a sea lion never sat the other way, for there were always enemies, the old ones taught. Daniel kept his distance. Goshun fixed all who approached with a wide-eyed stare, and for the remainder of the lull tide and on into the time the waters swelled for long tide, Goshun just lay on the moss, his breath heaving in and out with unintelligible sounds. At times his eyes were open and vacant; at other moments, they were half-lidded as if his thoughts were far from this cove.

Daniel did not know how old Goshun was, but certainly he'd seen the cycle of thirteen moons more times than there were digits on his flippers. Hagis and Achitopel sometimes doubted that the fat old bull could once have been the tribe's beachmaster, but Daniel believed in Goshun's past glory. There was pride and power in the old one's bearing—or maybe Daniel just liked the white-fur because he'd looked kindly on Daniel's attempts to shape treasures, had understood the part those objects were meant to play in the Singing.

Blossom and Esther gave maddeningly incomplete accounts of the battle in which Goshun had lost power to Tashkent. On the one flipper, they would tell the younger sea lions about the fight, and how much stronger and fiercer Tashkent had been than Goshun—but when Daniel asked questions about the time of that fight, which was always referred to as "before the typhoon," the older cows wouldn't answer him directly. "Why do you want to know about that awful time, Daniel? Everything's all right, here," the cows would say. "Have another piece of cuttlefish."

Yes, Daniel thought, as he swam his usual hundreds of leisurely laps around the cove in mid-afternoon, the past was confusing. He tested the viscosity and aeration of the water at various depth levels. He located a current that he could ride to stay below the surface for many laps on end without coming up for air. He could do more undersea laps without surfacing than any other sea lion in the tribe.

On his circuits he came close to the edge of the walls' opening, and could feel the coolness of the water out beyond the cove. He fancied he could even sense the presence of sharks and killer whales, those seldom-seen creatures who roamed the outer ocean just waiting to catch and devour young sea lions. It was forbidden to venture past the edge of warm water. No actual barrier prevented the tribe from leaving, but, as Esther often said, "a safe sea lion is a live sea lion." The cove gave the tribe warm water, regular food, ample perches, and protection from outside dangers. "What more could a sea lion want?" Blossom was fond of repeating.

Daniel wanted more. It would be exciting to go beyond the walls. Thirteen moons ago he'd been too small to think of going out, but now he was bigger and stronger and wiser. He'd tried to interest Hagis and Achitopel in a joint venture, but they just laughed at him, so he stopped telling them his dreams. He didn't want to be considered foolish. Anna knew of his desire to go, but he'd sworn her to silence.

There was a recent addition to the cove, in the north

wall, beneath the waterline: an undersea cave with a glass front, where bipeds often gathered to gaze at the tribe. Karl was in there now—Karl, the dominant biped, in his red-and-blue coverings—and Daniel did a tight circle of welcome. Karl fed him wafers in the evening, and Daniel liked him—but he didn't understand bipeds. Why did the descendants of the ancient biped Kanonah like to watch sea lions so much? Why, when bipeds entered the water, did they put on sea-lion-like coverings—black flippers and sleek skin? Of course Daniel was grateful to the bipeds for having rescued the tribe from the great typhoon, but, just the same, bipeds were an odd race of creatures.

At the surface, Hagis came by with a round, airy toy given to him by a biped watcher, and the young bulls played with it for a while, joined by Zelda and Marlena, two cows from their birth cohort.

Daniel caught sight of the great bulk of Goshun's body and didn't want to play any longer. The old white-fur was obviously in difficulty. He'd pushed himself to a more comfortable position, now, but still had not regained the Whistler's Shelf. Daniel moved onto a low ledge nearby, where, with his flippers still dangling in the water, he could observe the old one.

Goshun acknowledged his presence with a snort. Alone among the older tribal members, Goshun appreciated the little treasures Daniel made for the dying sun. Daniel told him, in a low voice, about the treasure he had made today, and that he hoped to have it honor the sun. Goshun snorted again, and then stopped. His eye shifted across the cove, to where Tashkent was stirring. Daniel turned in that direction. The leader swam slowly and purposefully across the cove toward them.

"The beachmaster approaches," Daniel murmured to Goshun.

"Not a real beachmaster," the old one growled. "We live here like otters! 'No surrender,' I told him! But he pushed me off."

Daniel was shocked and intrigued. Tashkent not a "real" beachmaster? Living like otters? "No surrender"—to whom? He had no time to guess, for Tashkent loomed in front of him, the parallel scars on the leader's back standing out in the bright sunlight.

Tashkent's voice, which seemed to come from the depths of the cove, growled a warning to Daniel to leave that perch so Tashkent could claim it for his own. Because Daniel didn't move instantly, the voice roared, and the great teeth sliced the water in an unmistakable threat.

Daniel was scared of Tashkent. In the past, when the leader issued orders, Daniel had always given way. But there were plenty of other perches where Tashkent could sit; they were just as comfortable, and unoccupied.

"Why must you have this perch?"

"I want it," the leader said, his voice low with menace.

Daniel didn't budge.

Tashkent withdrew and started to circle the cove. This meant a fight was coming. Circling was a well-known signal. Most problems between bulls were settled through threat of force, not by actual fights. In the distance, Daniel saw Hagis waving a flipper, telling him to move now, before something bad happened. As a rule, Daniel didn't like fighting, but something in what Goshun had said about Tashkent made Daniel stubborn. He'd have to fight. Maybe it was time. After all, he was bigger and stronger and maybe even a little craftier than he'd been six or thirteen moons ago. His teeth were sharp from working on the wood. He might have a chance against the dominant one.

Tashkent approached at high speed and leaped out of the water at Daniel. But Daniel had expected this approach, and, at the last moment, threw himself sideways off the perch while twisting his head and baring his teeth. The two bodies flashed by each other. Daniel's teeth caught the older bull's ear and ripped it half off. Tashkent slammed into Daniel's former resting place hard enough to hurt himself, and roared with rage. Blood streamed from his ear. In the water, Daniel swam for the deepest part of the cove, where he'd have the greatest latitude for movement. He'd need it to escape any second attack. So far, he'd been lucky. His only injury was a scrape along the flank, which didn't slow him up at all.

While he waited for Tashkent to make his move, Daniel pondered Goshun's earlier remarks. He longed for an explanation of why Tashkent was not a "real" beachmaster and how sea lions in the cove were too much like the despised otters, but he dared not approach Goshun. The Whistler's Shelf was too exposed; there, Daniel would be vulnerable to any new Tashkent charge.

Half a tide passed without either Daniel or Tashkent changing their positions, except for Daniel coming up now and then for air. When the blood stopped flowing from the leader's ear, it was almost full long tide—time for the Singing.

Once a day the crash of the waves against a dual rock formation at the edge of the southern wall produced a humming sound of remarkable pitch and loudness. It seemed to mimic a call made by a sea lion, and had a lot to do with the tribe's affinity for this particular cove. How could any sea lion not love a place that, itself, rendered honor to the dying sun?

Daily, during the ceremony, the Whistler would lead the tribe in songs, accompanied by the sounds of the Stones. When the sea swallowed the sun, then day was finished and it would be time for night. This day, however, as the Stones began to hum, old Goshun didn't heed their call. Atop the moss-covered slope he rasped, seemingly unable to move into position to lead the ceremony.

The breach of procedure upset Daniel, and he swam near to see if the old one was alive. It was just at this moment that Tashkent surprised him—not by attacking directly, but by moving toward the Stones and Bright Corner. Using his superior size and strength, Tashkent leaped up at Daniel's storing place for the treasures— which the leader could reach at any tide—and started to smash everything in sight.

Over and over again the big bull rose up and grappled the ledge, crushing the abalone shell, the trilobite in amber, the delicate little saw, the driftwood that Daniel had so carefully shaped. Helpless to prevent the leader's rampage, Daniel slid back into the water.

Daniel watched as the fragments scattered over the water, then sank, adrift on the currents. His work was reduced to pebbles, shards, and sand.

As the sun's reddish rays bathed the cove, Tashkent's laugh boomed through the encircling walls, and was cruelly echoed by the humming of the Stones. The other bulls and cows picked up the sound and soon they, too, were barking with merriment at Daniel's expense. The leader swam to Blossom and allowed her to lick the blood from the wound to his ear, which his exertions had reopened.

In midcove, Daniel sank rapidly toward the bottom. Down here, at least, he would not have to endure the laughter of the tribe.

2 · THE LEGEND

Sitting on the bottom, Daniel tried to shut out the memory of his ruined treasures by thinking about the concerns of the Singing—the eating of the sun, the endless sea, the old verses about Beachmaster Saul.

Finally, he decided to risk Tashkent's wrath and surface for the end of the ceremony. He came up only to discover that there was no Singing. Goshun was too ill to lead it, and no one else would. However, Goshun was speaking, and Achitopel, Hagis, Anna, Zelda, Marlena, and others of Daniel's birth cohort were gathered at his flippers, listening. Goshun lay on a ledge, his body shivering, his untrimmed whiskers wafting in the breeze. Daniel joined the group.

"And so," Goshun said in a wavering voice, "and so Beachmaster Saul gathered his bulls around him and made ready a fierce attack upon Mandragar, beast of the hundred tentacles."

"Hundred tentacles or hundred testicles?" Zelda asked with a smirk and a flirtatious twitch of her hind flippers. The other young sea lions chortled, and even Daniel had to smile. But then the import of what Goshun was saying hit him.

"Quiet!" he ordered. "It's a new part of the legend— one we've never heard before."

"Oh, Daniel, who cares?" Marlena said. "He's old, he smells bad, and his words make no sense."

As she dove into the waters, she yelled, "Last one to Grunting Cave gets no partner!" All the others followed her, except Anna, who stayed behind with Daniel.

"Isn't this great—a new part of the legend!"

"Something about a stray rockfish, perhaps, Daniel?"

"Look, Anna, I'm sorry about last night, but—"

" 'But it was so interesting, I just had to chase it,' " Anna finished for him. "Your dreams are nice, Daniel, but if you want me to share in them, you're going to have to pay more attention to me. Can't be swimming off every time something intrigues you."

That was what he loved about her—the observations that were always so accurate. Usually her shrewd eye and tongue were put to good use on other sea lions and conditions in the cove. Turned on him, they hurt! He felt a bit ashamed. He'd make it up to her, somehow—but couldn't she see that his heart was racing?

"I said that I was sorry. Go ahead with the others. I'll be with you in . . . in a half-tide, at most."

Anna sighed at him, and sped away.

He'd have to endure the ache, because he simply had to question Goshun on these new fragments of the legend. For many moons Daniel had struggled with the verse in the Singing about Saul:

> *Deep, the realm of Beachmaster Saul,*
> *Great-great-grandfather of us all;*
> *Dark, Pacifica's storied walls,*
> *Yet still the monarch sounds his call:*

"Come, lions that dwell in the sea,
We travel far in mystery!"

It had been Daniel's questions about Saul that had brought him closer to Goshun. The old one had actually confessed to Daniel that he didn't know everything about the legend; the result, he said, of being an accidental rather than a chosen whistler. Before the typhoon the legend had been passed down from whistler to apprentice in an orderly fashion. The storm changed that. With both the whistler and apprentice killed, Goshun, as the oldest sea lion, was then forced to assume the duties of chief of the singing. But he remembered only phrases and fragments of the story that both he and Daniel loved.

As best Daniel could puzzle out the legend, there had once been Pacifica, a home cove where the sea and land mixed equally. In Pacifica all of the earth's principal creatures dwelt at peace—the bipeds, led by Kanonah, and the sea lions, led by Saul and his mate, Selchie. There were hints that Pacifica had come to a terrible end:

The stars drowned, the sun shed its skin,
The ocean rose high, the land fell in . . .

As with many of the verses Goshun sang, these were maddeningly incomplete. Daniel believed that the next fragments recounted how unending rains made the waters creep up around Pacifica until all the land creatures were threatened. If the earth were underwater, only the sea creatures could survive. Soon on the land, only

Kanonah himself was alive, clinging to a tree on a high mountain. From that perch he begged Beachmaster Saul to carry him until dry land reappeared. The sea lion and the biped made some sort of agreement—Goshun's verses had no information about it—and then Saul, who was very large, swallowed the biped and carried him within his belly for a complete cycle of thirteen moons, and then, when the waters receded, spewed Kanonah out on dry land.

Kanonah was initially grateful to Saul for having saved him. Then came his treachery. The biped stole Selchie and took her on the land to mate with him. Their union produced land creatures of great variety, which she fed with her wondrous milk; in this way, the dry parts of the earth were repopulated. After this, the brokenhearted Saul took other sea creatures to mate, and thereby sired many tribes of sea mammals. However, the sea lions themselves, having lost both their Great Mother and their ancient home, were forced to roam the ocean in eternal search for food and shelter. Seldom did they spend more than a moon or two in one place, and today many sea-lion tribes fought continuously with the bipeds, and, of course, they no longer spoke a common language with the descendants of Kanonah.

At the heart of the singing was the verse that insisted that sea lions were doomed to roam forever—or

> *Until the spirit of Saul returns,*
> *Until the time of one who learns,*
> *Until the sun in darkness dwell,*
> *Until Kanonah's pups do sea lions tell.*

Tell what? And how? It made no sense to think about a day when the sun lived in darkness! And how to find Pacifica, which was buried somewhere beneath the sea, guarded by the fearsome Kratua, a beast whose very breath flamed the ocean? The whole legend was a riddle that perplexed Daniel as much as it fascinated him.

There was one part, though, that seemed to hold out hope: the mention that the spirit of Saul might return.

"Goshun," Daniel whispered to the old white-fur, "tell me more about the Great Beachmaster."

"On the day of the typhoon, the mothers died," Goshun growled. Daniel groaned. Goshun was talking, but not about countless cycles ago: This was a story from Goshun's own younger days.

"When the mothers died, there was no milk, and a great sadness was upon the waters." Goshun's eyes teared, and he muttered, "No pups born since then; no pups in this cove."

Well, Daniel thought, at least that was true: He and the others of his birth cohort, who had survived the typhoon because of the bipeds, were, indeed, the youngest members of the tribe. But even they were several cycles old, and almost fully grown now.

On the far horizon, between the outstretched flippers of the cove, the sun touched the sea. From various points around the cove, sea lions watched in silence as blood-light spilled from the dying sun onto the waters and clouds. The sight of the sea eating the sun never ceased to amaze Daniel. Now, only Goshun seemed unable to appreciate it, and Daniel wondered if, in his agony, the old bull had at last gone blind. Poor Goshun!

Was there no one to notice Goshun's problems but him? Looking around, Daniel saw part of the reason: It was feeding time. On the escarpment, Karl and the other bipeds appeared, carrying baskets of fish. A feeding pack of sea lions formed, led, of course, by Achitopel, who was on the verge of becoming fat. Daniel saw that Karl also had a box of sweet wafers with him; many of the tribe crowded around Karl, because all sea lions loved the wafers. Under the waterline, the fire-givers, so thoughtfully placed on the walls by the bipeds, started to spread warmth against the approaching evening.

There would be time to eat later, Daniel thought, and turned back to the task of urging Goshun to tell more of the story of Saul. Daniel began to chant:

> "Thirteen, the sons of Beachmaster Saul!
> Listen, lions, and name them all:
> Dairmuid, Zorn, and Achitopel,
> Hagis, Daniel, Popocatepetl,
> Goshun, Lokat, and Tashkent—"

"Urrrgh!" Goshun burped. "Tashkent not real beachmaster!"

"Has he made us live like the lowly otters?" Daniel asked, trying to irk the old one into saying something new. Goshun's mind seemed to clear. He faced the young bull.

"Live like otters, too close to shore. There were days, youngster, when sea lions were truly lions of the sea!"

"Tell about them."

Slowly, Goshun began to speak of endless moons on the ocean. He told of a "region of ice" where the days were never warm—a region inhabited also by descendants of Saul, but not by sea lions. Daniel's head thrilled at the idea. Goshun immediately switched to talking of other matters, equally mysterious: of a friendly shark with teeth for eyes and a boulder for a head, of the spirit of Saul returning, perhaps residing in the heart of an unnamed one who would win the right to be called beachmaster and lead his tribe to glory.

Wasn't a shark always an enemy? How could there be a place that was never warm? And what tribe held that unnamed hero, the new beachmaster with the spirit of Saul? Daniel longed for answers to these questions, but Goshun had fallen silent.

"Wouldn't you like something to eat, Goshun? I'll bring you a nice, soft flounder, and we'll continue—"

"No food," the white-fur said, with a low growl. In the vanishing twilight, Daniel was unable to see if Goshun's eyes had any spark.

He wished the old one would talk forever, tell everything about life beyond the cove, about the legend and the time when his kind had truly been lions of the open sea. Behind him, in the cove, the tribe became more jovial; a result, Daniel knew, of gulping down the sweet wafers. A few sea lions started singing mating songs—the early evening's complement of bipeds liked that, all right.

"How about a wafer?" Daniel asked Goshun, and repeated the phrase sea lions usually said to one another about the wafers: "It'll make you feel better."

"Poison of the accursed bipeds," Goshun howled. "Worse than the red tide—death of the mind!" He thrashed about.

Daniel was shocked. Of course sea lions had an age-old grudge against the sons of Kanonah, but still, hadn't bipeds rescued Goshun's own tribe from the typhoon, and daily brought the colony food, warmth, and wafers? Shouldn't Goshun temper his anger with gratitude to Karl and his helpers?

"Belly-up," Goshun said softly. "Soon go belly-up."

"No!"

Goshun die? Impossible! It would be terrible if he died. There had been two ugly deaths in Daniel's time in the cove. Two old cows, they were; they'd bled uncontrollably from their mouths after eating something that had been thrown down by biped pups. When the cows had gone belly-up, Karl and the other bipeds had descended from the cliffs with nets, and had taken the cows away. The cows were never seen again, and, afterward, no one spoke of them—especially not to the younger sea lions.

Goshun must not be allowed to die. Daniel suddenly realized how deeply he cared for the old one; now he must act on his feelings. Twisting his body, Daniel splashed cooling water onto Goshun's face. The old one seemed refreshed by the water, but he continued to speak about death. When Beachmaster Saul had died, Goshun said, there had been an important ceremony. A cadre of bulls had decorated the leader's upturned belly with colored stones, then towed him out to sea, where his body drifted on the currents until it was consumed by the dying sun. Every sea lion, especially every beachmaster, Goshun avowed, ought to have such an ending.

"But, old one, you're not going to die!"

The moon rose. Full, round as the sun and nearly as

large in tonight's sky, the "female light" lacked only the day's golden heat. A shiver passed down Daniel's spine. Under the moon's colder, smaller eye, Daniel could see males and females of the tribe pairing off, going to dance and mate. This evening, for the first time, he had not eaten food. And he wouldn't mate, either. To shut out the sights and smells and sounds of the tribe's pleasures, he climbed closer to Goshun, whose voice was fading.

In bursts of sound obviously made at great cost, the old bull whispered directly into Daniel's ear. The younger one strained to understand, could not always do so, and succeeded only in retaining the words so he could later puzzle over them. What were ice floes? The eternal hunters? Hauling out? In what sense was a beachmaster something more than just the dominant male of the tribe?

"Tashkent, ungrateful pup!" Goshun murmured.

"What do you mean? Is he *your* pup?" Daniel asked, unable to contain his surprise.

Goshun sighed, as if far away. "That's all for now, little one. Go ask your sire." Then, except for his rasping breath, Goshun said no more. He seemed to pass over easily into sleep.

Daniel didn't budge from his side. Thoughts crowded in on his mind like sea gulls to a beach after a violent storm. Was Goshun saying that Tashkent was his son, and that Tashkent was Daniel's sire? Impossible! Disgusting to contemplate!

The broken-shell bits of Goshun's stories were exciting, but they also were upsetting. The more Daniel learned, the more there seemed to be to find out. Once he'd thought he knew what it meant to be a beachmaster;

now, he wasn't so sure. Once he'd believed that to mate with a female was satisfaction enough; now he wondered about siring pups. Once he'd understood that Beachmaster Saul had lived in the ancient past; now he felt certain that the beachmaster's spirit was alive—somewhere!—in the present.

"Daniel," a female voice called to him, "Daniel au Fond."

Was the moon herself calling him? He turned to find Anna staring into his eyes. Her own eyes were larger than he'd ever seen them, and they shone with the reflected glow of the moon. Last night he and Anna had loved. Then he'd been foolish enough to leave her and go chase a rockfish. Now her body weaved back and forth in a dance, and her slurred voice asked him to accompany her once again—all past problems, presumably, forgiven.

"I've a secret to tell you," Anna said softly, "and I won't say it out here in front of everyone." She glanced at the snoring Goshun.

"I'd like to share your secret," Daniel said earnestly, "but Goshun's very ill, and my head is so full of strange thoughts right now that I don't know if—"

Daniel abruptly stopped speaking, because, behind Anna, Hagis appeared and playfully pulled her down into a breaking wave. Anna's imploring eyes held Daniel's in their grasp. He rose on his foreflippers in a threat posture, but Hagis used his bulk to push Anna away from the ledges.

"Wanna make somethin' outa it, Dan'l?" Hagis growled, then burst out laughing.

Daniel knew it was the wafers talking, not his brother,

and so chose not to square off and fight. Hagis shouldered Anna in the direction of the far side of the cove.

"Spineless cuttlefish," Anna hissed at Daniel. "Interested only in yourself!" She and Hagis swam away, into the darkness, toward Grunting Cave.

Anna's remark wounded Daniel, and he lay by the snoring Goshun, thinking dark thoughts. The moon passed behind a cloud and stayed out of sight for some time. The cloud changed shape, from mackerel to octopus to wafer to Anna's eyes. Daniel strained to stay awake so that if the old bull fell during the night he could help.

By the time the tide had changed again, near moonfall, a plan had made itself known to Daniel. He would leave the cove. He'd take Grandfather Goshun, and together they'd solve the puzzles of the old legend, and maybe even find the spirit of Beachmaster Saul. Could he "travel far in mystery"? He wondered what it would be like to fight a Mandragar, to move in regions of ice, to swim for a day in one direction and never reach a wall, to sire a son and a grandson.

3 · LEAVING

Just before the sun was born again from the mountain, a faint glow in the eastern sky woke Daniel. Asleep! He hadn't meant to doze off. He missed something and, for a moment, couldn't figure out what; then, he knew—the sound of Goshun's rasping breath was gone. In the gentle waters of the cove he saw the belly-up body of the old bull floating, its great bulk billowed by the waves. Slipping from his perch into the waters as quietly as he could, Daniel approached Goshun. There was nothing to be done. Goshun was dead.

Tears welled unbidden in Daniel's eyes. He blinked them back and nudged the old body into the lee of Elbow Overhang, where it would be out of sight of the sea lions on their sleeping perches and the bipeds on the back escarpment.

He dove to the bottom to think. Just at the moment he had understood that he had a grandfather, the grandfather had gone away. Despite the old bull's harsh manner, Goshun had been his friend. What would Daniel do without the old one? Goshun had no one else to mourn for him, and Daniel felt inadequate to the task. A broad sadness engulfed him; he could not shake it.

The idea came to him: He would take Goshun's body out to sea and give it to the sun, as bulls of old had done for Beachmaster Saul. The thought cheered him, and he began to work with a purpose. He placed stones under Goshun's flippers, in his mouth, and on his upturned belly. These, he discovered, made the body completely neutral in buoyancy, so that it could be pushed along on its final journey with a minimum of effort.

On the bottom he located a great prize: In the pedipods of a starfish skeleton, an agate had lodged. The sea had done this work, but Daniel had a notion to make it better. Chewing out the desiccated center of the five-pointed star, he forced the agate within, so that it entirely filled the central mouth cavity. The result was a treasure of surprising luminosity.

He was just completing this task when Tashkent appeared near the Overhang. The leader looked at the dead Goshun and grunted.

Daniel concealed the star beneath his flipper. Tashkent eyed him briefly, then turned away.

Unable to keep his thoughts to himself, Daniel said loudly, "At least he won't have to live like an otter anymore."

Tashkent whirled about in the water. "Watch your mouth, youngster. You don't know what you're talking about."

"Don't I?" Daniel retorted, his eyes hot with anger. "Would you leave him so that the bipeds could come down with their kelp lines and make him vanish as if he were a piece of waste, like one of the metal worms they're always throwing in and taking out?"

The leader's voice was oddly soft in response. "His spirit is gone, Daniel. His body won't care what happens to it."

"Will you mourn Goshun?"

"What I do is my business, and the tribe's," Tashkent said, his manner once again gruff. He glided away.

Daniel was shaking. Moments later, Anna swam by, as if only idle curiosity had brought her near Goshun and Daniel. She looked wonderful this morning.

"Is he dead? I heard no splash."

"You were busy at the time he fell."

"Mmmmm. I did ask you to dance with me first."

Daniel acknowledged that with a grunt that was not unlike Tashkent's.

They were both silent. The wind picked up and slapped the waves more sharply against the Elbow. On the rocks at the foot of the escarpment, three bipeds were changing their shapes. They must have spotted Goshun's body, Daniel thought, as he watched their hands become flippers and their skins darken and become tight and slippery.

"Anna," Daniel said quietly, "I have to go now—go out of the cove. I'm sorry for anything I did that wasn't to your liking."

"Apologies aren't the problem, Daniel, it's—"

"Anna—could you come with me now?"

"Outside? Right now?"

"Yes. I must give Goshun's body to the sun." He started to push the old bull's decorated body through the eddying currents and out toward the opening of the encircling arms. Anna swam alongside of him, but seemed undecided.

"We could get killed out there."

"Yes, that's true. But we could also be fine."

"I don't know, Daniel. . . ."

"Look, I'm going. This is something I have to do."

"Oh, that's ridiculous. Who's making you do it?"

"I'm not sure. I only know I must."

"If this is so important to you, Daniel, then go ahead," said Anna. "Do whatever it is you're bound on doing. I'll see you when you return."

"I don't know when that will be."

"No more than a half-tide, I expect—or you'll catch your death of cold."

The swimming bipeds came steadily toward them. Daniel calculated that he might not reach the opening of the cove before they did if he expended any more breath talking with Anna. The agate-starfish slipped off Goshun's body in an unexpected gust of wind. He caught it in his teeth and passed it to Anna.

"Keep this star," Daniel barked. "I'll come back for it, and for you. Look at it and remember me, Anna!"

"Daniel!"

The bipeds in sea-lion coverings were only a few lengths away. Daniel turned for a last look around the cove. Was Tashkent laughing? Urging him on? He couldn't tell. Daniel accelerated with every muscle in his body, and nosed the carcass of Goshun past the edge of the cove's walls and into the cold waters of the endless ocean.

〰〰〰

Only a few dozen strokes of his flippers beyond the cove, Daniel was amazed to discover that the rocks which had for so long been his home were only a small part of a larger shoreline almost as endless as the ocean, stretching north and south as far as the eye could see.

Two hundred lengths from shore, out beyond the biped floaters, the waves themselves changed character. Their peaks were higher and their troughs were lower. They were also more widely spaced, and not all angled toward the receding shore. The most curious thing was that the waves did not move him at all; only his flippers could do that. Inshore waves, he concluded, had pushed him along on their crests, but these ocean waves passed right through him, lifting him up and down in one place without pushing or pulling him forward or backward.

For all its buoyancy, Goshun's body was hard to steer to the sun. Daniel became warm with the exertion. This was dangerous for a sea lion, because excess heat threw the body out of balance. Daniel thought the cooler waters would help, but they only made the problem worse—he was both hot and cold at the same time, and started to shiver. He slowed down, hoping to get his body back to normal heat. Maybe a westward current would relieve him of his burden.

Undulating vibrations from something below made his whiskers tingle. Looking beneath the surface, Daniel made out a school of smelt going by at an angle. He'd never seen so many live fish in his life! Since he hadn't eaten last night, he was extremely hungry. Letting the old bull float alone, he dove straight at the small silver fish. They scattered in all directions, their scales reflecting the overhead sunlight. He was dazzled and confused by their motion, and his mouth came up empty. On his next dive he maneuvered to separate several of the silver streaks from the larger mass of fish, then hunted these down before they could rejoin the others. He ate one under the surface, using his reserve air supply; two more he brought up and slowly savored. They were delicious—entirely fresh, full of blood. Compared to these, the long-dead mackerel provided by the bipeds at the cove were stale. How could he have eaten them, all these moons? While digesting the smelt, he returned to the task of pushing Goshun. A half-tide later, Daniel sneezed, and his throat spewed out the bones of the fish, which sank toward the bottom.

In the far distance, he caught sight of some enormous silver fish. For a moment, they seemed to be huge shadows of the smelts he had killed. The far-off phantoms spouted water—though he wasn't sure how—and occasionally leaped out of the ocean and sliced back in as they traversed in a generally southward direction. How did they do that? They seemed so carefree, so beautiful. Daniel had no strength to investigate them at the moment.

Still hungry, and feeling less as if he'd die from heat loss, he dove again for food—and was surprised when he saw no fish whatsoever, in any direction. He was also amazed to find the sea so deep underneath him. Usually, in the cove, his dive would carry him effortlessly to the bottom. This time, the bottom was so far down that he had to push hard to reach it. When he got there, it looked different to him than the bottom of the cove—dark, murky, filled with odd projections and objects. Looking up, he could hardly see the sun. On the bottom was a bivalve clam that was similar to those he'd occasionally seen in the cove—except that this, too, was gigantic, almost half his own length. Was everything in this ocean so vast? Hungry though he was, he didn't dare try to eat something that large. He came up.

At the surface, he burst out into a laugh: The ocean was so grand, at once incredibly full of creatures, and terribly empty! The size was scary, but exhilarating.

Goshun had drifted, and Daniel nudged him back on

course. The sun was high in the sky. To the northwest, clouds had begun to gather, but they were far away. In back of him, eastward, the coast was only a faint blur at the edge of the sea. He caught sight of the mountains only when a wave lifted him high enough to be above the usual surface.

A chill went through Daniel. This time, he figured it out: He was losing heat too quickly to the cool sea. Going slowly was not the answer. He had to generate more heat internally, or stop moving and lie in the sun. He decided to speed up and hope to make a landfall while the sun was still in the sky. But where? Far above, he saw a bird, a lone sea gull, heading slightly to the northwest. He altered course to follow it, knowing gulls did not stray far from land.

Moments later, he caught the scent of a group of sauries—small yellow fish that sometimes leaped out of the water in their attempts to eat surface insects. He was thinking about going after them, when, thirty lengths to his south, a large gray shape appeared. Instantly the sauries scattered in the opposite direction, then switched back eastward as they sensed what Daniel soon saw to the north—another gray shape, a shark.

A memory came to him. One day at the cove a shark had appeared at the edge of cold water, and, before anyone could do anything about it, had ripped apart a young female sea lion. Her screams had filled the air and attracted Karl. The biped had come with a stick that threw fire and noise at the shark, and killed it, though too late to save the young female sea lion. There was good reason for the elders to warn the youngsters about sharks.

After Daniel had made ten more flipper strokes, there were five sharks nearby, their bodies beneath the water but their dorsal fins showing just above. They slowly circled Daniel and the carcass of Goshun. On each circuit, the sharks seemed to move closer to Daniel. No matter how swiftly Daniel pushed the now-bloated body along, the sharks kept pace.

They came closer. He could see the shriveled skin of the dorsal fins, he could see the shadows of pilot fish that shifted and turned with the great beasts as they writhed through the waters, he could see the rows upon rows of ripping teeth. Daniel was afraid.

"Go away!" he yelled at them. If they understood, they didn't obey.

One of the gray beasts came swiftly toward him, and, before Daniel could sense precisely what was happening, it tore a chunk out of old Goshun's haunch. A trail of blood drifted out and became a black-red cloud beneath the surface. Instantly the other sharks turned in the direction of the carcass.

Five of them! Coming at him!

Daniel collapsed his lungs, closed his nostrils, and dove—dove with surging power and with hardly a notion of where his dive would take him, other than away from the sharks. Down, down, down Daniel went, far enough so that at the bottom of his trajectory the light was dim. Even so, he could feel, far above him in the waters, the sharks feeding in a frenzy. All about him, the ocean filled with clicks and vibrations and moans, as thousands of creatures nearby warned each other to flee far from this spot until the monsters had sated themselves.

Grateful that the sharks were not following him, Daniel surfaced several cove lengths away, and streaked toward the blood-red sun. Highlighted against it was a small dark dot—an island! He made for that.

As he flew through the water, he realized that Goshun's body as bait had been the last of the white-fur's legacy to him, Daniel thought—a gift of escape from instant death by the sharks. It was companion to Goshun's other gift, the vision of the legend of Saul, which freed Daniel from the lingering death of the mind in the cove. In dying, the old one had bequeathed life to his grandson: That, surely, was the mark of a beachmaster, and Daniel was glad he had honored Goshun as one.

4 · ALONE

Daniel au Fond woke to the first bright rays of the morning sun. He turned toward their source, saw the golden-red circlet rising out of the sea—and was astounded. Where was the mountain that, each dawn, had given birth to the sun? The orb was so low in the sky, sitting on the waters!

Looking about, Daniel realized that he was on a spur of rock at the tip of a small craggy island. All the muscles in his body throbbed from yesterday's exertions. To hop about, even to think of swimming was difficult. He clung to his tiny projection, just above the spray of breaking waves, and gazed in all directions. He saw nothing. On the eastern horizon the blood-gold sun was squeezing up into the sky, but elsewhere, there was nothing but water. The island itself was no more than an outcropping of rocks set precariously into the sea, home to tiny, ugly crabs, some slugs and sea snails. A half-dozen terns and an albatross dotted the upper, jagged rocks of the island's center. He saluted them with a bark; even though they were only a length or two away, they did not scatter, knowing that they were out of his immediate reach.

A hard, isolated place, this island of small crabs.

In the cove, not half a moon ago, he'd spent an entire day gathering treasures on the bottom of the cove and had been scolded for staying by himself more than befitted a sea lion. He'd fancied he liked isolation—but now, in mid-ocean, without the accompaniment of a single other sea lion, he felt truly alone. He missed kamarla, that time each day when the whole tribe would huddle together, bodies overlapping bodies, minds at rest, when each sea lion knew in his or her bones that the tribe was more than the personalities of all the individuals in it. He missed feeling that oneness.

"Well," he announced to the birds, "there's nothing to be done about that except to return, and I want to have a few adventures first."

The island's crabs were so small and had such hard carapaces, that they weren't worth the effort of smashing. But he was hungry and so, with grunts and groans, Daniel dragged his way to the edge of the rocks and hopped off into the water. Cold! A shiver went through him, but after a few dozen strokes, his body began to adjust; in a way, the chill eased his aching muscles.

Beneath the surface the island sloped away downward, at an angle, in all directions, and Daniel concluded he'd been sleeping atop a mountain. Nosing toward the depths in pursuit of some small, gray-yellow fish, he made the mistake of brushing against the long, translucent tentacles of a jellyfish. Instantly, his left foreflipper swelled in size and throbbed dangerously. He was forced to return to the surface and haul himself onto the island to wait for the swelling to go down, which it did by midday.

After that incident, he was more careful in the shallows. Some of the desirable fish hid beneath jellyfish, while others stayed near the almost-as-poisonous sea anemones. For fear of being stung, he could neither swat those fish with his flippers nor grab them easily in his teeth. He moved farther out from the island, though he stayed on the recognizable slopes of the undersea mountain. A storm was approaching from the northwest, and he didn't want to be caught too far from shelter.

Underwater sounds and vibrations revealed a small school of tomcod. Streamlining his body, Daniel gave chase—mouth open, nostrils shut, whiskers alert, flippers aligned for speed. The first fish he caught was the largest he'd ever held, almost as long as a flipper. He clamped his jaws on it tightly. This was a mistake, as its strong muscles writhed and the fish was soon free. Daniel lunged after the tomcod again, and this time held it more loosely in his jaws, taking it to the surface, where the fish's struggles only exhausted its energy. He ate it in three sections.

Hunting had many other surprises. He hadn't realized how carefully the shape and coloring of the plaice and flounder resembled the ocean bottom. He had to work hard to find them when they hid on the ocean floor. Trying to creep up on a plaice, Daniel almost got his hind flippers caught by an enormous clam as its shells started to close. In the cove, feeding had been neither hard nor time-consuming; out here, it was both. A whole tide passed before he was able to fill his belly.

By then the storm was quite near. The sea's surface changed from bluish to green, and was roiled with whitecaps. In the vicinity of the island, eddies and crosscurrents made swimming difficult. There was an odd, brilliant allure to the sun, which dipped in and out of the clouds, threatening to disappear completely at any moment. Then, quite suddenly, the sky darkened to the color of shark.

He had to get to safety.

Daniel clambered on the little island and wedged his body tightly between two boulders. He was three lengths from the edge. The birds had fled, the crabs had gone into crevices to hide. He saw no other creatures. The air filled with a soaking rain. On the horizon lightning burst. A few moments later the noise of thunder reached Daniel. Almost as quickly, there was a second shock of light, so close that it dazzled his eyes and the thunder vibrated his whiskers. As waves smashed higher and higher over him, the distinction between sky and sea vanished. Locked against two pillows of rock, he was buffeted by the attacking waters. After a dozen heavy blows, he realized something was wrong. The sea was rising—overtaking the land, as in the legend. How had Beachmaster Saul survived? By staying in the water! Of course: To remain here would get him knocked senseless. Gauging a trough between two waves, Daniel dove into the ocean and streaked diagonally down the side of the seamount as far as strength could take him.

A dozen lengths below the surface, the sea was calm, untroubled by the winds clawing the world above. Daniel settled to the bottom to wait. Slowly, deliberately, he willed the flow of blood to his hindquarters to thin. His windpipe and rib cage had already collapsed, and he did not breathe out or even lose air in bubbles. His heart slowed. Lub-dub. Lub-dub. Lub. Dub.

Darkness. Cold. Immense waves. An image grew in him, a throb of unexpected pain: He was being fed milk by a large female as he lay close to her—and then, all of a sudden, he was being tossed about on a sea so powerful he feared he'd go under forever. He called for help from the mother who fed him and kept him so wonderfully close, but he couldn't find her anywhere. Lost, he was utterly lost! Where was she? He felt sick, his belly swollen with unwanted water. The waves tossed him up and down and terrified him. He was tired. He wanted to sleep but couldn't or else he'd drown. He screamed. More blackness. More water in his belly. Then the waves quieted, the darkness gave way to a hazy light, and he was able to see. All about, there were belly-up sea lions and countless dead fish. Was he dead, too? Where was Mother? Who were these creatures in floaters standing on hind flippers? How did he get into the air, lifted by a power not his own? Looking around, he saw kelp lines carrying other sea lions into the floaters and felt the shock of impact on a hard surface. The upright hind flipper creatures moved toward him. Held him. Put a nipple in his mouth. Warmth. Calm. Milk. Quieting flippers, comforting smells. He wished to have kamarla, not to think at all, just to be. He felt grateful to the new creatures. Thankful. Small. Alive.

At the bottom the sand swirled, obliterating the seascape. In the hazy depths a creature appeared; its many arms moved over the undersea mountain, a large mass of flesh coming toward him. Mandragar, Daniel thought. But was the beast in his memory, or present where he was now? He fought to emerge from his trance, but knew he could not surface yet, for the storm was still blowing. Three lengths away from him the armed creature wrapped its countless tentacles about the bivalve clam that earlier had almost gotten Daniel. The thing seemed to caress the clam, to settle over it completely. Some time later—in his befuddled state of mind Daniel couldn't tell precisely how long—the creature unwrapped itself and moved on. Only the clam's gaping and empty shells were left behind. As the beast passed by, Daniel moved, and, in response, a cloud emerged from the thing, a fearsome blackness that made the water into night. Daniel struggled to pump blood into his extremities, to flee from the darkness, but as he neared the surface in panic, he felt pain in every joint of his body and had to go back down until he reached a level at which the pain—and the panic—subsided. Next time he'd be more aware of the depth, so he could rid his bloodstream of danger before coming up from a lengthy dive.

~~~~

During the next moon he stayed close to the island, each day venturing from its rocks to practice dives, hunt, and collect little treasures such as a glass bubble, wood with designs on it, curlicues of bones. He followed flocks of birds when he discovered they would lead him to schools of fish. He figured out how to attack a school so that the fish would be unable to avoid his slashing teeth. He found that octopuses would not attack him if he gave them enough room, and trailed in their wake at the bottom, locating crannies where crayfish had secreted themselves. He developed techniques for flushing even the most crafty flounder and plaice from the protective nettles. He stayed away from the prowfish that lived under the stinging tentacles of jellyfish, and swam away from crabs that held anemones in their claws.

None of this experience was acquired lightly. Each night he nursed some wound or other—a scrape from a coral, a puncture with a nettle spine in it that would have to work its way through the flesh of a flipper and out the other side. However, injuries seemed to heal far more quickly out on the ocean than they did in the cove. His skin became toughened. His fur thickened; after half a moon, the morning's first plunge into the waters no longer produced shivers.

He grew used to being alone and proud of his adventure. He was Daniel au Fond, son of Tashkent the Terrible, grandson of Whistler Goshun, descendant of ancient Beachmaster Saul. He was in search of Pacifica, the lost home of his race, and of the spirit of Saul which was alive somewhere on this vast ocean. Perhaps, when he found the new beachmaster who would embody the spirit of Saul, he'd apprentice himself to him, and hope to learn what the qualities were that made a sea lion a true and great lion of the sea.

5 · STRANGE GRAZING

O n a calm, clear morning, Daniel au Fond swam away from Small Crab Island, heading south. Behind him on the island was a collection of stones and wood, crowned by a glass floating ball: It would identify the place for him, should he return.

His measured, steady pace kept the coastline occasionally in view on his left. By midday his pace had exhausted him. He tried sleeping on the waves, curled into a tight circlet with foreflippers and hind ones touching. For a quarter-tide the troughs and peaks lulled him, but the rest was unsatisfactory. He had to stay alert for sharks and other predators, and couldn't completely relax. He saw the outline of another small island, and went ashore. Quickly he dropped off to sleep. When the sun was on its slide into the sea, he awoke, refreshed, eager to hunt and play. He sang his own song to the departing sun, then dove into the darkening waters to look for fish.

His eyes widened, and he discovered he could see quite well even though the sun was no longer above. Swimming thirty feet below the surface, he learned that the fish that had been unreachable and below him all day in his travels had now migrated up toward the surface, and were above him, dark against the lighter sky. Now they were easy to capture. Moreover, some of them seemed to give off their own faint light, which distinguished them from the sea's blackness, and all he had to do was go after these lights to obtain a meal.

From that day on, he traveled only part of the day, slept during the hottest tides, and hunted at twilight and just before dawn. After a few days of this, he realized that life in the cove had proceeded on a schedule set by the bipeds, not by the tribe.

As he swam south, he concentrated on acquiring knowledge from the sea around him. Many of the sights encountered on his journey were new and quite wonderful. He was excited by the lightning-bolt pattern on the elusive halaconda fish, by the softened metal and wood of an old biped floater that had sunk to the bottom of the sea, by a group of moving islands on the horizon that turned out to be whales. He tried but couldn't catch up to them. One night, he used a pointed stone to scratch a lightning-bolt pattern into the wooden side of a sunken biped floater.

Other things he encountered on his travels were not so pleasant. One day, veering far out to sea to avoid some floaters that made a great deal of noise, he entered the edge of an area of unusually warm water. Pursuing the warmth, he dove quite a distance below the surface. Down below, the sea was dark, not only because he was far from the sunlight; an opening in the sea floor, far beneath him, was continually spewing forth material. For a moment, Daniel wondered what it had swallowed, since it was spewing up so much. As he approached, the water became warmer and warmer; soon, it was too hot for him to go any closer. He could make out the opening but couldn't get near it, because the waters surrounding it were bubbling with intense heat. He was astounded to catch glimpses of creatures that survived there: They seemed to be distorted versions of common fish and undersea dwellers—one had immense jaws but virtually no body, another was a group of numerous octopus-like tentacles that waved in the currents, a third was a gigantic worm, a fourth had countless eyes. If these creatures made him afraid, how would he feel in the presence of Kratua, the monster who guarded Pacifica?

Nearing a bleached sandbar at low tide, he saw the staring, whitened skeleton of a large creature. He stopped to examine the bones, because he had never seen bones as big as these—intact, without flesh. They must be quite old. Though it frightened him, he was able to hop around and even through sections of the skeleton. Part of it was like an open cave that must have held the belly and heart of the animal. In front there was something like a piercer on a spearfish. From the arrangement of the bones, it was clear to Daniel that the creature belonged neither completely to the land nor to the sea. Parts were adapted for swimming, others for moving over solid ground. After a half-tide, Daniel swam away from the sandbar, as he'd fled from the area of hot and black waters.

These images from his journey came back to him in his dreams, swirling about like the eddies of remembered whitecaps, mixing with deep currents of the legend of Beachmaster Saul.

He used the time at sea to practice maneuvers he'd attempted in the cove but never had proper space to work on. He streaked along in one direction without changing his path, at about two lengths below the surface, until his breath was exhausted—and was amazed to discover he'd traveled the equivalent of hundreds of laps around the cove. During another experiment he closed his eyes and tried to swim at one depth just by feeling the temperature and currents with his body; this he found he could do quite accurately, and it helped with his night hunting. He worked on extending his capacity for diving, until he could go down without hurting himself, to where there was no sunlight and the pressure was intense. He perfected a power push that enabled him to leap out of the water with a graceful and elegant motion. The first time, he leaped over a startled school of sauries, and scared up an instant meal.

Having perfected these maneuvers, Daniel knew that he'd become the best swimmer of his tribe, that he'd gone far beyond what any of the individuals in the cove had ever attempted. For a moment, contemplating this achievement, he was elated. Then, thinking about it awhile longer, he became profoundly bored. Of itself, perfection was a silly goal. For the first time in weeks, Daniel felt alone again.

Before he quit any of his temporary homes, Daniel fashioned markers with stones, wood, glass, shells, and other objects. He didn't simply accumulate the pieces and leave them in a pile, but spent entire mornings augmenting the designs and scratching patterns into his treasures.

At times, while traveling, he would wonder: Is this the adventure?

One day he followed a flock of sea gulls toward an area near the horizon, anticipating easy pickings—mackerel, or some crunchy smelt. "How's the weather up there?" he asked the flight leader. In answer, he received a hail of droppings from the whole pack, and went under to avoid being spattered.

When the birds settled to the surface and Daniel caught up to them, he found that they were floating in a patch of sticky, black, viscous ooze. There were mackerel, all right—dead ones, belly-up in the muck. Daniel felt queasy and avoided the patch as best he could. The birds stayed right in it, though, ate the fish, and got the ooze on their feathers.

"How can you eat that?" Daniel barked at the gulls.

"Hungry. Eat," said one. "No wriggle, no wriggle," said another, delighted that the fish weren't moving.

"You're getting that stuff on your wings," Daniel warned. "How will you fly?" There was no answer. Some of the gulls began to strangle, because of the ooze. But the others didn't stop eating. "You birds are being stupid," Daniel yelled at them, hoping, at least, to provoke a reaction. Maybe he could lead the birds away from this danger. But the gulls ignored him and kept eating, even though it was obvious to Daniel that they would soon die. With a shudder, he hastened away from the black patch.

Waking on a small island one day, he saw waterspouts not far offshore, and, imagining they came from the beautiful silver swimmers that he'd seen before, was eager to join them. But he saw quickly that the spouts were not those of the graceful, playful dolphins he'd spotted earlier. They were from other creatures. Sensing danger, he returned to the island's safety. The spouts of these large black and white creatures were being used to herd some bonito toward the shallow water near his perch. Fascinated, he watched the attackers, who were two or three times his own size, as they closed in on the bonito. The hunters made a loose semicircle that stretched around the bonito. Then, to make the circle smaller, they swam in toward the island, spouting all the while. When the bonito had crowded into the shallower waters, one of the attackers put on a burst of speed, slipped beneath the water, and emerged a moment later with an entire big bonito crosswise in his jaws. With a snap, the black and white attacker closed his jaws, and the two halves of the big fish fell back into the water.

In a flash, the others came in and killed a half-dozen of the frightened bonito. Daniel could hardly believe the rapid pace and thoroughness of the killers. That's what they were, he concluded: killer whales. The name was apt. He stayed on the island that entire day, until the creatures had disappeared beyond the horizon.

Next day he came upon a few fronds of kelp, and started eating it. The taste was good—he realized he'd missed it, in his steady diet of fish—but these fronds were dead, having floated off from the main bed. He followed them through the waters near to the mainland, where a group of the enormous leaves grew in a shallows. Little crabs, shrimp, and other crustaceans clustered on the fronds, and it was great fun to wrap the leaves around himself in the water and then break them. He wished Hagis were here to play tug-tug with him. Enmeshed in the fronds, he didn't notice the approach of a group of swimmers until they were almost upon him.

"Ahem," said one of them. Daniel turned about and saw a large silver dolphin whose wide-open mouth made him seem as if he boasted a continual smile. "Excuse me, you're transgressing on our territorial prerogative here."

"Huh?" Daniel said. He was astounded that these other creatures could speak, and he didn't quite understand all their words, though he recognized most of the sounds.

"My place," the silver fish said with exaggerated slowness. "Belong dolphin. Me dolphin. Me big."

"There's plenty of kelp here for all of us," Daniel said. The fur on his neck began to bristle.

"Attend to the little squirt," said another dolphin. "He talks!"

The first dolphin responded with a toss of his head and that awful smile. "It's not really very smart to quarrel with us, sea lion." The other dolphins swam close around their leader; in doing so they effectively screened Daniel from the main part of the kelp bed.

Daniel grunted and, without really thinking about it, made a feint and dove down twenty feet. Then, at the bottom, he turned and started up with all his power, rising into the maneuver he'd worked on. His jump carried him over the leader and into the fronds. The move surprised the outspoken dolphin. Others of the silvery ones laughed in high squeals.

"Hey, Percival," chortled another dolphin. "I think the sea lion's not impressed by your admonitions." Percival's lips clamped tight over his teeth, then he lowered his head and charged—right at Daniel. Daniel felt a sharp blow to his nose and was knocked backward. When he recovered his senses, he was bleeding from the nostrils.

"What'd you do that for?" Daniel said. "I didn't attack you, did I? There are five of you, and I'm alone."

Percival edged next to Daniel. "My apologies for the excessive use of force," he said, "but our experience with sea lions has convinced us that they are usually quite rude. And stupid. You, obviously, are an exception. How did you manage that vaulting?"

"What's it to you?" Daniel attempted to stop the bleeding by lowering his nose under the surface of the water. The inner membranes closed, and the salt in the water made the wound swell and shut off the blood flow. He took some satisfaction from that.

"Perhaps you might want to join us," Percival said. "We're rather pleasant companions when you get to know us."

"I'm on a quest for something that has nothing to do with dolphins. Besides, I don't need any help. I'll make my way by myself." He started to dash away.

"An admirable sentiment, lad," Percival shouted after him as Daniel sped south. "Look me up when you've come to despise being alone!"

He cautiously continued southward for two more days, staying closer to the coastline. Near high sun on the third day, as he was digging in a bottom bed of mussels, he saw what appeared to be a familiar silhouette twisting and turning above him. Could it be? He rose to the calm, glassy surface and saw a most beautiful young red-coated female seal.

In the tribe the old cows had told a tale to the effect that Beachmaster Saul had failed twice when he began to sire offspring. The first was too large—a walrus. The second was too small—a seal. The third was a sea lion, whose size was "just right." Seals were unlike the members of Daniel's tribe in that they had no external ears and their hind-quarters were more tail-like and fused. This seal was smaller than he, and more graceful in the water. Her pelt shone, her body was sleek, and her eyes were clear.

"Ha theah," she said gaily to him, turning over on her back to drift on the tide. Around her neck she wore an ornament that sparkled in the sun. "You-all new in these pahts?"

Her voice was like her body, musical and strange. He wanted to speak to her, but was so charmed by her presence that his mind couldn't form words. Signaling with a flipper that he'd be right back, he dove to the bottom. A succulent little flounder was lying near a staghorn coral, trying to be invisible. He grabbed it and brought it, still flopping, to the surface.

"Lunch," he offered.

"How thoughtful," she said sweetly.

They spent the afternoon swimming in sight of the coast, and getting acquainted. A biped floater was nearby all the time, but Daniel paid it no attention. The seal said her name was Helen, that she lived not far from this spot, although her tribe hailed from farther south. She was out for a lonesome swim because she preferred to be away from the crowd and their boring antics. The necklace—given to her by a friend—was delicate and unable to withstand pressure, so she couldn't dive too well. She was appreciative of Daniel's ability in that undertaking. Yes, she had heard in her youth that all seals and sea lions were descended from Beachmaster Saul.

"Ah remembuh some stories about him ridin' some enormous wave."

"I don't know that one."

As they swam nearer the beach, the rapidly rising sea-floor and the push of the ocean threw up a marching line of big breakers. Helen showed him how to ride one—such a thing had been impossible in the cove where Daniel had grown up, and it had not occurred to him to ride breakers while out on the ocean. Daniel soon mastered the motions necessary, adding the wave's power to his own and shooting through the waters at great speed. The trick was to move along the curl of the breaking wave, not quite at the top but in the grasp of its surge.

They played with the breakers for a long time, until the sun itself was racing along its descent toward the horizon. Daniel hadn't had such fun since he left the cove; it took more than one—seal or sea lion—to capture the excitement of a game like riding the waves.

"Uh-oh, Dan'l—look out!" Helen shouted.

Daniel had been lolling on his back, using only his hind flippers, waiting for the next big wave. Helen shoved him, and he turned over and dove, just in time to avoid a biped floater speeding toward them with a great deal of noise and urgency. It seemed aimed right for them! A metal, whirling set of teeth passed over his head, close enough for him to feel its awful vibrations. The floater sped off, and Daniel swam back to Helen's side.

"Ah'm glad yoah not hurt," she said. "Those bahpeds kin be vicious."

"They could've killed me."

"Poah deah."

"You know about bipeds, too?"

"Mmmmm." Helen started toward the beach with a

push of her hind flippers. "Getting late," she called. "Race yuh t'the fah beach."

Using her more fishlike hind flippers, Helen burst away from Daniel at a speed greater than he'd imagined she possessed. It took effort on his part to follow her, and he only caught up with her on the rocky beach after an exhausting sprint. There they both lay, breathing heavily. Beyond, the breakers crashed and mists of spray momentarily obscured the sun. Far above, on the cliffs, there were biped houses.

Never had Daniel felt so excited by a female, and, as they sniffed and nuzzled around each other, Helen seemed equally interested in him. As the sun sank into the sea, he mounted her and they mated until moonrise. Then, exhausted, Daniel fell asleep, one flipper resting on her haunch.

Kelp lines dropped over him and he awoke. A moment later, the lines lifted him in the air. A fleeting vision of the rescue in his youth passed through his mind. He was swung onto a vehicle by bipeds. He cried out for Helen, who was climbing onto the vehicle by herself. A biped put a clamshell in front of her, and she ate greedily from it as another biped stroked her red-brown fur. There was a loud noise, similar to that made by the whirler of the floater, and the vehicle started moving through the night. Daniel jounced along in it, helpless in the tangled kelp lines. Dulled, not able to fathom what was happening to him, he could only think to ask Helen what she was eating.

"Caviar," she said.

Part Two

BEING TESTED

6 · THE LABORATORY

*T*wo of the walls were glass, and the back of the triangle, the third wall, was white stone. All went straight up, several times as high as Daniel could leap, and at the top were open to the sky. A three-length-deep, six-length-long pool took up most of the space between the walls; its water was tepid, clear, and tasteless. Urine and feces that Daniel passed into the pool disappeared through a metal opener in the bottom.

Set in the back wall was a small cave where he could not be seen by the bipeds. Near the cave's entrance were layers of smoothly curved ledges on which a few strange objects were arrayed: a series of sticks and egg-shapes attached to other sticks. There was a glasslike window in which lines and patterns appeared and disappeared. Daniel understood none of these things, and would not touch them. He did very much want to talk to Helen, to find out why she had led him into captivity—for there was no doubt in his mind that there was no way out—but Helen was nowhere in sight, though a faint smell of her came from beyond the wall. The only other living beings Daniel could see, hear, or smell were bipeds wearing white coverings; they walked on their two legs just outside his area, and glanced often at him.

Daniel was alone, and frightened.

By the second day he was also bored and hungry. Needing to do something, he decided to pull down on one of the sticks with a foreflipper. Instantly, a meaty little sardine came out of a place in the ledge. Daniel gobbled it up and pressed the stick down twice more. Two sardines appeared, and he ate them. Still hungry, he pushed the stick up and down many more times, until there were enough sardines to satisfy his hunger.

Later in the day, when he pulled the stick once more, no food appeared. Wandering, he came to the pattern glass with the egg-shapes on sticks attached to it. Inside was what seemed to be the shadow of a clamshell, but he couldn't grasp it with his teeth. Was it a real clam or just a dream clam? As he moved closer to examine the glass, his flipper hit the egg-shape. Instantly a shadow of a small rock lobster appeared in another part of the pattern glass. Thinking that all he had to do was pull the egg-shapes and sticks, Daniel then touched a stick near the food outlet, but received, instead of food, a sharp pain in his flipper. He jumped back. Turning around, he saw the bipeds outside watching him.

For a while, he stayed as far away from the pullers and egg-shapes on sticks as his confines would allow. Then a notion intrigued him. Approaching the patternmaker, he pushed an egg-shape, and the shadow of the rock lobster changed to that of a mussel. He pushed it again, and it was now a clam—brother clam to the one on the other side. Cautiously Daniel moved to the food stick and pulled at it. This time there was no shock. A clam popped into the food area.

"Ha," Daniel muttered to himself, "even a sea gull

could figure that one out." He cracked open the shell and gulped the clam. As long as he was trapped here, he thought, he'd have to play the silly biped games. Well, all sea lions loved games, so perhaps that wouldn't be so bad.

Once having decided to work steadily with the egg-shaped sticks, and patternmaker, he made great progress. The problem of producing two shadows he mastered quickly. Then it became a matter of three.

When the shadows were of clams, lobsters, and the like, the task was simple. Any sea lion could have done it, Daniel thought. Soon, however, the task became more difficult. To avoid the pain that was sent to his flippers when he did the wrong thing, he had to match shapes that were different from any he had ever known. He struggled a bit with this, but worked it out. No matter if a shape was familiar or not; if its contours matched the others, then he could identify and find a partner for it. As he managed this task, he saw several more bipeds gather outside the glass walls. Now he was having fun. Three squiggles. Three suns divided by half-floaters. Then noises were substituted for the shapes. It took him a while to figure that out, but, once he'd done so, he was able to identify the noises. After that, the things that required matching were combinations of sounds, smells, and sights.

By day's end, Daniel was exhausted. He missed not being able to see the sun being swallowed by the sea, and he sang a low, mournful tune to remind himself of the breaking waves, the odor of the horizon. Falling asleep easily, he nevertheless dreamed of triangles attacking him and of mackerel that vanished when he went to bite them.

Next morning a white-coated biped entered the pen and

stood on the ledge where the games were, moving his hands in a peculiar manner, making the same motions over and over again. Angered at what he'd had to endure, Daniel ran at him with teeth bared. As his mouth was about to close on the biped's flesh, Daniel heard a high-pitched noise, and, a moment later, felt a great shock through the soles of his flippers.

That day was the most harrowing of his life. For the longest time he could not understand what the biped wanted. Repeatedly, he encountered the high-pitched noise and the shock that followed—until, at last, he grasped the idea that he was to do what the biped's hands ordered him to. He was to jump in the water. Come out. Approach the biped. Stay where he was. Roll over. By late in the day he was receiving fewer shocks and more fish for his efforts. In addition to learning when to jump and when not to do so, he also came to understand the hand orders for pressing certain sticks and egg-shapes in sequence. It was after moonrise when the biped himself brought Daniel his dinner, a nice variety of inshore fish, some of them quite young and tender. When the biped put his hand out to touch Daniel, however, Daniel growled and whirled about, showing his teeth. The biped's hand was withdrawn.

That night in his dreams, Daniel swam among a bevy of sharks and killer whales that became biped hands ordering him to shock himself.

Next morning, he had to do everything all over again. He did. He was pleased with himself. At the urging of the biped, he climbed to the top ledge on one side of his pen. A door slid open in the white wall, and Daniel peered into the adjoining space. It had a larger pool, water that smelled enticingly of the sea, an area of complicated sticks, egg-shapes, and other gadgets—and Helen.

"Congratulations," she called. "You made it through the fust stage, and ver-uh quickly."

Daniel hopped into Helen's space, but stood silent, whiskers alert, wary now of new places and seals who were ver-uh charming.

"Aren't you comin' enny clos-uh?"

"Not after last time," Daniel snorted.

Helen laughed. "Don't be a fool. Ah've done you a fav-uh by bringin' you heah." She climbed out of the pool and onto a ledge near him.

In response, Daniel dove into the waters. The pool was salty, buoyant, full of tiny motes of marine life. After he'd had a comforting swim, he came out, shook his fur, and lay down.

She waited until he was dry, then offered to show him around. He grunted and did not move. Ignoring the fact that he was snubbing her, she trotted off toward the area with the extra sticks and egg-shapes and pieces of strange materials. It was right in front of a glass window that was partly open, so that bipeds could look in and make sounds, too. Helen stuck her head through the window opening and let the bipeds groom her.

"Fred's awful nice," Helen said, indicating one biped with glass near his eyes. Daniel grunted again.

"Puzzle tahm," Helen said. At a small ledge she set to work with her flippers and teeth in an attempt to connect two long, hollow sticks. After a while, impatient at her lack of insight, Daniel shouldered her aside. He inserted one hollow stick into a hole in the ledge which seemed made for that purpose. Then, with his teeth, he picked up the other stick and jammed it into the top of the first. Because the ledge held the first stick solidly Daniel was able to force the connection.

The bipeds clapped their hands, showed their teeth, and made happy noises. Helen shrugged. Daniel accepted a clamshell of caviar from Fred, but still growled as Fred's hand touched his fur. The hand was withdrawn. The new method of combining sticks, Daniel decided, would be useful if ever again he was out on the ocean and could make a treasure.

Intrigued by the possibilities, Daniel spent the remainder of the day with Fred, solving the other puzzles. Helen sniffed at him angrily as he separated clamshells by size. She went to sulk in a corner as he used a stick to open a closed container and then sorted by weight and shape the contents of it. When Daniel located certain objects at the bottom of the pool and brought them to the surface, then arrayed them in a design that matched one the bipeds had laid out, Helen spewed fishbones on Fred's clothing.

It was dark above when Fred signaled farewell, the lights were turned off outside the pen, and the bipeds left. Daniel was weary. A half-moon and some colored dots on the bipeds' machines provided the only illumination. Helen appeared sad. Unable to contain himself, Daniel asked her what was the matter. She told him that if he continued to swim through the puzzles as swiftly as he had this day, he'd soon surpass her. He looked at her with comforting eyes, as if to say that had he known, he would've gone slower—but he thought in his heart that he shouldn't have gone one bit slower.

Too excited by his progress to keep silent, Daniel asked

Helen some more questions. Yes, she replied, she'd been in captivity for some time, and had passed a whole lot of tests. These tests? Well, no, not exactly, but some difficult ones. And she was allowed certain freedoms.

"Going back to the ocean, you mean?"

"If you weah a necklace," she sniffed.

It occurred to Daniel that her comments implied that other seals or sea lions had gone through this testing process. Correct, she said. And where were they? She wasn't sure, but thought they might be on the new floater the bipeds had just hauled in.

So much information in one day! The idea of a floater was intriguing, for it held out the possibility of escape. However, Daniel suddenly couldn't muster up enough energy to ask about it. He decided to sleep.

When Helen rubbed her whiskers against his in a provocative way, he was confused. Hadn't Helen betrayed him once already? Didn't he have to maintain his isolation so he could be ready to escape and continue his quest? Wasn't she dangerous? Well, yes—but there was no denying that Helen was beautiful. At last he decided that coupling with her would be good, so long as he didn't put all of his heart into it.

7 · THE FLOATER

A half-moon later, Daniel saw his reflection in the pool. Twice Helen's size, almost full-grown, he was larger than he'd remembered. He had scars—a slash from Tashkent, various stings and cuts, a patch of fur he'd torn away himself by scratching at a place where the black ooze had clung to him. His nose was askew from having been butted by Percival. Helen often told him that the imperfections of his body were a record of his journeys; she liked them.

Even though Fred was part of the biped tribe that kept him in a cage, Daniel was beginning to like him. Fred wouldn't shock Daniel unless he failed to do a task correctly or deviated from the straight path to the goal. If Daniel performed well, he was given food and Fred scratched him behind the ears. Back in the cove, Karl had smiled at him, fed him, and, in a sense had allowed Daniel to think of himself as free; he understood that Karl's cove had been as much a trap for sea lions as Fred's laboratory. In fact, he preferred the laboratory, because at least Fred's intentions were always clear.

One morning Fred and two other bipeds entered the area Daniel shared with Helen. Before either Daniel or Helen could figure out what was happening, restraining kelp lines had been attached to them. Then, by hand signals, Fred directed them into a biped vehicle, which made a noise and started to move. As they traveled over the land in this vehicle, Daniel looked out and felt the wind ruffling his fur; he calculated that they were moving at a speed far greater than he had ever made by himself on the ocean, a pace too rapid to allow him to fling himself out of the vehicle. To try an escape now would be to risk mortal hurt.

At the edge of the ocean the vehicle came to rest. Daniel was full of joy to see the water. The back of the vehicle was flung open, and he and Helen were led onto a white floater. The bipeds held the kelp lines and directed them into an area atop the floater that had a small pool with ledges leading into it. Waiting in the pool were two seals.

"Hullo, boys," Helen said gaily, "nice tuh see y'all again."

Banta and Blog were from her own tribe, red-skinned and sleek, larger than Helen, though not so massive as Daniel. From the way they nuzzled her, Daniel could see that Helen had known them for some time. She'd probably helped capture them, too, and in the same way.

The floater moved out to sea. Daniel was thrilled. Sitting on a high ledge atop the pool, he inhaled the ocean smells deeply, and felt in his bones the throb of the floater's whirlers as they worked beneath him. Fred came by and made the sign for "good job."

In the course of the next day, Daniel learned that there were many bipeds on the floater, as well as one very odd creature who went sometimes on two legs, sometimes on four. Smaller than the regular bipeds, though resembling them somewhat, he was also rounder, hairier—an orange color, actually—and rocked back and forth a lot when he sat down. His forelimbs were bipedlike, though almost as long as his entire body. He didn't chatter as the bipeds did, but he made hand signals at the bipeds and they answered back in the same manner. Blog said that the creature could speak seal—although he rarely spoke to them—and that his name was Sigmund.

Speaking with Blog and Banta, Daniel discovered that Blog had been trained on odors, and could identify the faintest traces of substances. Banta was able to balance objects on many parts of his body and to drag loads heavier than Daniel could imagine. On the other flipper, neither could equal his own skill at matching images or his dexterity in manipulating objects with flippers and mouth.

Helen, Banta, and Blog were all taken out of the pool the next day, and Daniel was left alone. The floater stopped in a small inlet. As Daniel watched in amazement, the bottom of his pool receded into its sides, and he could see the ocean floor a dozen lengths below. He immediately dove down to it, only to discover that metal kelp lines from the floater loosely surrounded him all the way from the floater's bottom to the seafloor. His trap had changed shape, and it was quite watery, but it was still a trap. Fred swam down to meet him. The biped was dressed in sea-lion covers, trailed a school of bubbles from his head and carried some strange devices.

During the next half-moon, Daniel spent most of his time in the watery trap at ever-increasing depths. He learned to locate and differentiate among various rocks on the seafloor and to perform certain tests on them down there. If he came across a rock that resembled a barnacle-encrusted oyster, he was to swim to a metal worm that had been lowered alongside him and find, in a series of glass eggs, one that held red liquid. Then he was to break the glass carefully so its contents poured on the oyster-thing. If that turned blue, he was then to carry all such oyster-things to another lowered metal worm and, by pulling the kelp line attached, to alert the bipeds above to raise it to the floater. There were similar procedures for other kinds of rocks—those that looked like the droppings the bipeds' dogs had left on the upper ledges of his home cove, those that lay flat like plaice, and so on. He especially liked the test in which the green liquid, poured on a rock, caused it to fizzle, bubble, and crack.

At first, during these tests, Fred was by his side; then, as Daniel grew more confident, he performed them alone.

At other times he swam outside the trap, but wore one of the same necklaces as Helen did, as well as a set of restraining kelp lines. Underwater, Fred held the ends of these lines, and made hand signals at him. "Come." "Eat." "Go fetch." The first time out of the trap, Daniel ripped the lines from Fred's hands with a mighty surge, and dove away ten lengths beneath the surface. He got as far as the end of the inlet before the necklace started to expand. Soon it had blown up to the size of one of the multicolored balls he'd toyed with in the cove. The ball pushed him to the surface where he lay, immobile, until the floater arrived and bipeds lifted him to the pool. On his next outings, he refrained from pulling the lines from Fred's hands. They swam about together—Fred was terribly ungainly in the water, Daniel noted. As the days wore on, Daniel also noticed that there were fewer and fewer lines on him. Then Fred held him by only one kelp strand.

Daniel guessed that shortly—tomorrow, probably—Fred would try to hold him without lines, with only the threat of the expanding necklace between him and freedom. Daniel planned what to do: at night, with his teeth, he'd secretly pierce the necklace in a place the bipeds wouldn't notice. Then, once he was in the water, the necklace wouldn't be able to prevent him from diving away from the floater.

That night he asked Helen, "Why do you stay here? You come and go without a kelp line. I could break your necklace for you, and we could swim off together."

"Well, the wuk heah isn't ver-uh hahd; besides, it's im-poh-tant."

"To whom?"

"To the bipeds. And to me. Ah lahk t'be . . . in control of the sit-u-a-shun."

Later, Daniel was unable to sleep. If Helen wouldn't go with him, he'd chance it alone. Suddenly Daniel became aware of the orange creature seated on a ledge above the pool. He had a fat stick in his mouth. As Daniel watched, Sigmund touched a metal rock to it. Fire glowed at one end of the stick, and smoke emerged from Sigmund's mouth. Daniel jumped back. Sigmund laughed—a high, eerie sound—and blew a circle of smoke, which floated away like a cloud. The moon was full.

"You learned that from the bipeds. Bipeds at my cove often put fire in their mouths."

"Very good, Daniel. This is called a cigar. Like to try one?"

"No, thank you, Sigmund—but, could I ask a question? You're not a biped, am I right? You're an animal, like us?"

"I'm not a biped."

"But you work for them."

Sigmund blew a smoke ring. "They are fond of me—they think I'm amusing—so they keep me around and teach me hand signals."

"At least you can talk back to them. All we can do is obey their orders."

"True." Sigmund nodded.

"Why should any of us work for the bipeds?" Daniel asked. The question had just bubbled to the surface of his mind.

Sigmund spoke slowly. "As smart animals, you and I can agree that most animals spend the better part of their lives pursuing food, sleeping, fighting, mating, and dying."

A lump formed in Daniel's throat. "Yes," he said hoarsely. "I've noticed that."

"There has to be more to life than that."

Daniel stood still. Sigmund's thought so matched his own that it took his breath away. How could this strange creature voice the very thing that had been bothering Daniel? The orange-colored one reached over for a glass egg of liquid, and poured something from it—a bit into a smaller egg glass for himself and some in a clamshell for Daniel. Sigmund sipped at his so Daniel lapped at what was in the shell. The liquid burned on the way down, but had a nice flavor, and it made his insides feel warm.

"Slowly," Sigmund warned. "Never gulp good brandy."

The night was beautiful, the moon round and full of mystery. Despite his captivity, Daniel felt happy: He'd found a new friend. They drank to one another. Daniel's head felt slightly dizzy.

Sigmund argued that bipeds were the smartest beings he'd ever encountered. Daniel nodded agreement. Sigmund suggested that work with the bipeds could give to certain superior animals the direction and purpose they otherwise lacked. Here, he said, was a rare opportunity to get beyond the repetitious, everyday drabness of life and use one's mind! Daniel wasn't sure what he thought about that, so he merely nodded his head, which seemed unreasonably light. Sigmund called it a privilege to perform tasks in association with the bipeds—he himself had been able to travel widely on sea and land, to view sights that no other animal had seen, to taste excellent foods, brandy, and cigars. Daniel's head was quite dizzy, so he didn't even nod at this. Sigmund pointed out that the things he'd done were beyond the ken of animals who had no help from bipeds. His hope was to one day learn to speak more directly with the bipeds; in better communication, he believed, lay the path to real partnership.

It was dawn when Sigmund left to go back to his own area. Daniel's head was as high as the clouds. To think that an animal could communicate with the bipeds! Maybe someday the sons of Kanonah would again talk with the sons of Saul! Today, it didn't seem impossible.

His thoughts continued along that line until, in the long light of dawn, he saw Helen's shadow rise and fall next to him. Looking at her, Daniel realized that she was a creature used by the bipeds to control other animals—even himself. The thought made him uncomfortable: A descendant of the Great Beachmaster ought not to work as a, well, as a slave for the descendants of Kanonah. That tongue of Sigmund's had almost convinced him how glorious it was to be in the service of the two-legged creatures. Yes, it was true that far too many animals spent all of their days hunting, but, no, it didn't follow that an animal's only purpose was to fill its belly. Sea lions could appreciate the beauty around them. They could follow the sun, have adventures, make treasures, attempt to improve themselves, even seek their destinies.

Daniel decided that by whatever means possible, and as soon as he could, he'd get away from the floater—else he'd be transformed into a creature like Sigmund, who was unwilling any longer to be content with what he was—an animal—and aspired to being what he'd never completely become, a biped.

8 · ESCAPE

~~~~~~~~~~~~~~~~~~~

*T*hat day, down below with Fred, Daniel had no kelp strands holding him—only the necklace. However, in the excitement of the talk with Sigmund the previous night, he had not gone through with his plan to pierce the necklace, and so could not attempt an escape. Curiously, Fred was more forthcoming than usual with small treats for Daniel. Later, atop the floater, Daniel and the seals overheard Fred and the other bipeds engaged in what seemed to be an argument.

After Daniel, Helen, and the two male seals had been fed their dinner, a great tiredness overcame Daniel. With some effort he managed to hop up to his usual perch, but then promptly fell asleep. He dreamed of bipeds bending over him, holding him fast, slashing at him with slim, sharp talons. He wanted to scream but had no voice.

In the morning his body throbbed with pain, and he discovered that the dream had been real. A disagreeable burning sensation hurt his left shoulder blade, and there was something pointing up from it that he couldn't quite make out in the mirror of the pool. Blog, Banta, and Helen also woke up with pain, and they also had things in their shoulders—round devices with metal whiskers. And their necklaces were now gone.

There was no work that day. Daniel spent his time gathering his strength, waiting for Sigmund to appear. The orange one might be able to tell him what the metal whiskers were. He avoided Helen as much as possible, but, in the confined area, that was difficult. Finally, she cornered him.

"Yoah goin' tuh leave," she said.

"How do you know?"

"A female kin tell."

"It's been a difficult time," Daniel explained, and put his head down. Helen started to lick at the place on his shoulders where the metal whiskers were implanted. It felt good. He couldn't quite reach back to scratch these himself. Later, their grooming led to more intimate embraces.

During the day, Fred came around, making greeting and friendly hand signs. Daniel ignored them, and the seals were too groggy to respond. Fred sighed and slowly walked away. He seemed sad, Daniel thought—just as if he were a real animal that had real feelings.

It was the evening of the full moon. Daniel sang a song to her. His shoulder throbbed and he couldn't sleep. After a while, Sigmund appeared, puffing heavily on a cigar.

"I've been waiting to talk to you," Daniel said. "Do you have one?"

"One what?"

"Of these itching things."

"It's not important. It sends signals to tell them where you are." Sigmund shrugged.

"Don't they trust us to come when they make hand signals?"

"No; I mean, yes, they trust you—the device is just to keep track if you get lost."

In spite of himself, Daniel laughed. Sigmund was spouting the bipeds' reasoning, not his own. As Sigmund moved, Daniel noted a signal sender in his shoulder.

"I see that you have one, as well. Does it hurt?"

"More deeply than the wound."

They sat together for some time. Sigmund had brought with him one of the little glasses filled with brandy. Now the orangutan looked at the biped object and flung it into the ocean. Though Sigmund said he'd remain a captive—he believed he had no real choice about that—he vowed to Daniel that he'd never drink the biped stuff again. Daniel felt sorry for Sigmund. He took him into his confidence, telling him about his planned escape and the blocked route out.

"Maybe another time will come," Sigmund said.

"The time is now. I want to get lost—that'll be a test of their metal whiskers, won't it?"

"They'll come after you, Daniel."

"If you help me, I'll have a head start."

"How?" Sigmund asked, leaning forward.

"There's that closer to the pool area . . ."

"The door?"

"Whatever you call it. Anyway, it can't be opened from the inside, but you could do it easily from the outside."

Sigmund didn't do anything for a moment, just sat there in silence, puffing on the cigar.

"I'll never forget you," Daniel offered.

"Wait to leave until I've gone back inside the biped cave," Sigmund said, and began work on the door. In a moment, it was open. Sigmund disappeared into the bipeds' area. Daniel waited until a cloud had passed in front of the moon, then nosed open the door. He was careful to do it quickly and quietly, and didn't allow the wood to slam back. However, the door did close behind him, and he realized he wouldn't be able to open it again. Even if the others had wanted to leave now, Banta, Blog, and Helen wouldn't be able to escape with him. He also hadn't said a proper good-bye to Helen—well, maybe it was better that way.

Metal sticks ringed the edges at the top of the floater. Daniel explored soundlessly, trying to find a good place from which to leap off into the water. At the very tip of the floater, where it was the most narrow, the metal lines did not quite come together. There was enough room for him to slip through. Standing on the edge, looking down, he almost lost heart. The floater was very far above the water, nearly ten times the length of a sea lion. Never in his life had he jumped from such a precipice. A badly angled dive might hurt him. But there was no choice.

Daniel flung himself off the edge of the floater and was suspended in the air for the longest time. He hit the water with little body impact, for his angle was good, but a great ringing went through his head. Also, just below the surface, the power of his plunge threw him against the metal kelp line of the anchor, which nearly crushed his right flipper. The hurts bothered him, but he embraced the ocean. He was alive, he was in the water, he was free of traps and balloon necklaces and bipeds!

By dawn, he was so far to the west that the coast was not even a faint blur on the horizon in back of him. He hadn't seen anything that belonged to a biped since moonfall.

9 · SARGASSO

W hen full light came up, Daniel discovered he did not know precisely where he was. Ten thousand lengths out to sea, he thought—but where? Out of sight of land, and having traveled at great speed during the night, he was disoriented. The wind had been at his back, but the waves at the surface didn't exactly conform to the wind directions, and, two lengths below, where he had traveled for most of the night, the direction was even further askew. There was nothing around him but deep ocean, and, while he was comfortable, it was a bit disconcerting to be that far away from land. The vastness of the sea gave him one comfort: Should the bipeds come after him, he would be able to see their approach from quite a way off, and dive to escape them. The metal whiskers in his shoulder bothered him still, but not enough to slow his hunting motions.

He was hungry, set about finding food, and searched for some time before happening on a school of dull-eyed pollack. One was enough for a full meal. After it, rather than swimming away, Daniel followed the fish as they meandered through the deep waters, rising and falling through the upper layers of the sea with them as they followed the smaller creatures who were their own food. Staying with the pollack, Daniel thought, would mean a continuous source of something to eat. At nightfall, he slept near them, a tight circlet atop the sea.

It saddened him to remember that he had not really sung of Beachmaster Saul in some time. The thought of the great ancient one had been an inspiration to him during his moons in the laboratory and on the floater, holding out the promise of escape and of pursuing his destiny. And yet, had those moons in the laboratory and on the floater truly diverted him from the task of becoming a lion of the sea, or were they part of the process? Certainly in that time he'd gained an awareness of the world and a knowledge of bipeds that might, someday, be helpful to him. He'd learned there was the possibility that sea lions and bipeds could communicate in some meaningful way. During his captivity, he'd confronted Sigmund and, in some senses, the bipeds, and had escaped to tell the tale.

During the days and nights trailing the pollack, the one part of his captivity he didn't think much about was Helen. He and the lovely red seal had gotten along pretty well, but something had been missing from their relationship. While in the laboratory and on the floater, he didn't know what bothered him about his female companion. Now it came to him: They didn't really talk to one another, not in the most intimate way. He'd never told her of his dreams, his failures, his small successes—never revealed to her how much he owed to Goshun, or how upsetting it was to have to face down Tashkent. He'd never told Helen a thing about Anna, mate of his youth. Anna was a secret too precious to be shared with someone like Helen—why, he'd sooner have talked about Anna to Sigmund, who wasn't even a sea creature. Anna. He'd like to see her again; he had a lot to relate to her about his journeys.

~~~~~

One day, Daniel noticed that the school of pollack had attracted predators other than himself—a bevy of sharks. He reluctantly decided to abandon the pollack and seek food elsewhere.

There were no clouds in the sky, and the sun brought a sizzling heat to the water's surface. Daniel was forced to travel beneath the waves for a long time without coming up for air.

As he came to the surface, he caught sight of some fish he'd never seen before—small, with brilliant orange, yellow, and black stripes. They hovered just at the tips of the waves, and their bodies shimmered with the sun's rays. Their school was slow, and Daniel had easy work catching them and downing them. He ate a half-dozen of the small fish before stopping to look around.

Not a quarter hour after having gulped down the multi-striped fish, Daniel's head throbbed and his belly turned flip-flops. The sun now hurt his eyes. Soon he began to wonder if he was seeing properly.

In the dancing points of light made by the sun on the water, fish flew through the air and birds swam upside down near the waves; a hoary bivalve with a beard of seaweed swung from a cloud; the clouds themselves formed shapes, altered them, and re-formed others with surprising swiftness. Daniel tried to hold tightly onto his mind as the ocean itself exploded.

Slowly the visions subsided; air and water separated once

more into the two halves of the world. But he swam now in what seemed to be a different ocean. Overhead, the sun stood still in the sky. The water was shallow, warm as his blood, and filled with creatures of all sizes—and all, as if lost, swimming in slow circles around a barren sandbar.

He searched for a way to get out of sight of the sandbar, which felt forbidding, but at the perimeter of the large circle there lay a wall of jellyfish, their tentacles dangling to the sea floor. No matter where Daniel swam about the circle, he encountered this formidable barrier.

"I guess I'm trapped here," Daniel said to nobody in particular.

On all sides, the water churned with fish—thousands of them, in every color of the rainbow and in varieties most of which he had never seen. He was hungry, but after the experience with the strange-striped fish, he was reluctant to catch and eat any of these. The same could be said of a blue-gray creature he saw trawling a hundred yards away, with its jaws closed tight and dorsal fin too high in the water for attacking position: Perhaps it, too, had had a bad time swallowing striped fish and didn't want to become further disoriented.

"That shape reminds me of Percival."

"At least someone here recognizes my distinct physique," said a high-pitched voice emanating from the blue-gray shape, which approached him at rapid pace. Daniel saw the familiar grinning face of the dolphin.

"Percival," Daniel sighed. "This is a dream brought on by bad food, isn't it?"

"Aha, you're the impudent young sea lion. Damned inconvenience, this sargasso, eh?"

"So that's what you call it."

An enormous killer whale crept up behind them, and, before Daniel was aware of it, was addressing them in a rolling, unwavering monotone.

"This, too, shall pass, Percival. And who might this lovely little morsel be?"

"Oh, Lavender—this is Daniel. How are you, old friend?"

Evidently the dolphin had swum everywhere and knew everyone; he must not be as youthful as his grin suggested. While the two renewed their acquaintance, Daniel tried to calm himself. Killer whales were frightening; on the open ocean, he'd swum from their attack. Yet here he was, flipper to fin with one, and she was quite friendly. Overheated, Daniel raised a foreflipper in the air and fanned himself with it. "Well," he remarked casually, "since we can't go anywhere, we might as well make ourselves comfortable. How did you get here, Lavender?"

The killer whale commenced a tale of being thrown off course during a typhoon. Percival countered with his story of having jumped so high out of the sea that the wind had blown him onto a cloud, and the next thing he knew, he was here. Daniel tried to top that, but his imagination wasn't so vivid. With a minimum of flipper and fin motion, the three of them floated together in the shallow waters, riding the currents in a circle about the sandbar.

Two more unusual creatures appeared, swimming out toward them from the sandbar. They didn't swim as real seagoers, but, rather, paddled with all four limbs like land animals. One was quite small, the other, large. The first Daniel thought must be an otter. The second was unknown to him, covered in white, shaggy fur. Daniel had guessed it was a quadruped, but when it reached them, it quite suddenly stood up on its hind legs, towering above them, several times the size of a biped.

"What a mess," the large creature said. "Never been in anything like this. I'm Esmeralda, by the way."

"Popocatepetl," nodded the otter. He pronounced the long name very quickly.

Upon hearing this, Daniel snorted—and was immediately sorry, as the others asked him to explain his rude action. He couldn't admit that he'd always been taught otters were inferior creatures, so he said, "I meant no offense, but that name is usually given to sea lions, as one of the thirteen sons of the great Beachmaster Saul."

"Saul also the name of my ancestor," the otter said curtly.

Daniel was puzzled—the more so when the gigantic Esmeralda, the white creature paddling through the shallows, said that she was a bear and that the name "Saul" was in her forebears. Could otters and bears be among the thirteen tribes of Saul? Was it possible that creatures so different from Daniel were all distantly related? Daniel sang for them the old verse with all the names—Goshun, Hagis, Achitopel, and so on. Percival recognized some names which were still used by his tribe, and so did Lavender the killer whale. Daniel's head spun with this information. They could all be the descendants of Beachmaster Saul! But that raised another question: Was Saul a sea lion, or something else? This was, indeed, confusing to Daniel.

While he was deep in thought, there came a babble of

squeaks from the far side of the circle, a noise of the sort that usually sprang from small fish as they were dying.

"What sort of misguided misfit could eat those miniscule morsels at a moment like this?" Percival wondered aloud.

All turned in the direction of the disturbance. A beast of immense proportions was flopping and charging about, crushing small fish in his mouth and not even swallowing them afterward. Daniel saw that the creature resembled all of them—shaped somewhat like a sea lion, though with forequarters more like a bear's, and with the same skin texture and tail as the killer whale or dolphin. It was the size of a true whale, and its unique feature was a single extended horn that came out of the center of its forehead.

"Does anyone recognize this incomprehensible configuration?"

"Not like anything that I know, Percy," Esmeralda said.

"Maybe it's dead," Lavender suggested.

"Then so are we all," Percival answered, because they could see the beast thrashing around the shallow waters, goring, biting, raking with its nails, horn, and teeth every life-form in its path.

"I think it's gone out of its mind," Daniel said. Awful though the beast was, something about it evoked a strong brotherly feeling in Daniel. He edged away from the others and called out to it to stop killing, to join with him and his new friends in trying to puzzle a way out of the present situation. The beast's response was a charge in Daniel's direction.

"Look out," Daniel yelled, and he, Percival, Lavender, and Popocatepetl sped out of the way of the beast's charge.

Only Esmeralda the white bear maintained her position, swiping at the creature with her great taloned paws. In return, it stabbed at her with the horn, drawing blood from her flank as it streaked by. Esme turned, expecting another charge, ready to defend herself—but the creature did not alter course. As if blind, it kept going until it reached the wall of jellyfish where, stung, it turned away. "Mentally unstable, all right," Percival muttered to Daniel.

"What he say?" the little Popocatepetl asked.

There was no time to answer. Esmeralda was shaking her body to rid herself of the oozing blood, and, beyond, the beast seemed ready for another charge. It was clear that the creature would destroy everything around it unless something was done.

"I don't want to die," Daniel said to the others. "We must do something." The others nodded, and looked at him expectantly. Why were they all peering at him? Certainly Percival was smarter than he, and Esme and Lavender were much larger. Why must he decide? And why did his heart go out to the creature, which, even as they debated, was senselessly destroying some beautiful coral formations that lay exposed to the withering sun?

"What ought we to do?" Percival asked him.

"We ought to combine our strengths to get rid of the danger," Daniel said firmly.

"Yes," Lavender agreed, "But specifically how?"

"Look—there are five of us," Daniel said. "The creature will attack any of us alone, even Esmeralda, but I don't think it'll go for two of us at once."

"It's starting to move again," Esmeralda warned.

Daniel quickly explained his plan. Esmeralda and Percival, as one team, would form up on the left, near the jellyfish, while Lavender was to interpose her bulk on the right. When the beast veered away from the jellyfish, both teams were to close in from behind and steer it back toward the center. That's when Daniel and Popo would start to swim in front of the animal—evading that terrible horn, of course—and lure it toward the center of the sargasso, the barren sandbar.

"At least we die together," Popocatepetl said with a shrug.

"Approaching momentarily!" Percival sang. Why was he so jolly at this moment, Daniel wondered—but there was no time to think about it. Everyone rushed to get into position. On the beast's pass outward it moved so close to Daniel that he could see several small fish impaled on its horn, and entrails of others dripping from its mouth. It wasn't even eating, just killing without reason.

"I scared," Popo whispered to Daniel.

"So's everybody else," Daniel whispered back. "Only a fool wouldn't be scared. Get ready!"

The monster approached. Beyond it were Lavender, Esme, and Percy, closing in to cut off its possible escape routes. Daniel and Popo started swimming strongly toward the sandbar, and the creature followed. On sighting—or, perhaps, smelling—the small animals ahead, it put on an extra surge of power, and Daniel had to strain to stay beyond the reach of the horn. He lost sight of Popo. As he sped through the water, scattering the fish, Daniel felt the bottom coming up swiftly. In a moment, his flippers brushed sand and rock. Reaching the sandbar, he didn't

stop but climbed out of the water and galloped swiftly across the barren sand. He was twenty lengths beyond the water when he heard Percy call him to stop.

He looked back. The creature had impaled its horn deep into the sand, and was flopping its rear parts about, helpless. Although it breathed air, its extremities didn't allow it to move on solid ground, so it was—as Daniel had planned—marooned on the sandbar. Loping carefully around the beast, Daniel went back into the water and was greeted by cheers from Percival, Esmeralda, and Lavender.

"Where's Popocatepetl?" Daniel asked, dreading the answer.

"Mmmmmfffggzz," said a faint voice on the beach. The little otter was struggling out of the wet sand, where the strange creature had trampled him. Daniel was glad to see him.

"Do you think the beast will die there?" Esme asked.

"In this heat? Rapidly, I surmise. In a quarter-moon it'll be positively skeletal, and in thirteen, all that will remain will be whitened bones."

Congratulatory conversation followed. Each animal assured the others that the beast could not have been vanquished but for his or her cooperation. Daniel agreed: There were some tasks that couldn't be accomplished alone.

So involved were the friends in re-creating the moment that they failed to note that the sun had moved more nearly aslant of them, until it was almost on the horizon. Then, at the periphery, the jellyfish began floating apart; there was a hole in the "wall" big enough for Lavender, if she didn't mind one or two little stings. Not only didn't Lavender mind, but said she'd widen the hole for the others. She wanted to leave immediately before she, too, could wash up on the sand. She left in the direction of the setting sun, scattering jellyfish on either side of her.

Esmeralda, the gigantic bear, was solemn as she looked Daniel in the eye. "At another time, in another place," she said, "I might not be able to be so gentle." Daniel nodded with understanding. Esmeralda swam away from the sandbar, heading east, and Popo followed. Only Percy and Daniel were left.

"Will I see you again, dolphin?"

"Though the seas are vast, the paths of the exceptional are remarkably intertwined," the grinning one said, and started for the south.

"That'll take me several moons to figure out," Daniel answered, even though there was no one there to hear. Swimming out of the sargasso, heading north, he twisted his head about for a final look at the sandbar. The great beast was breathing its last; its body lay in a heap on the beach. It would soon be a bleached carcass of bones much like the skeleton Daniel remembered passing on his first journey.

Had that glimpse of bones been a foretaste of this just-concluded adventure? Was this dead beast the ancestor of them all? Daniel could not answer these questions.

A true beachmaster, Daniel felt, would grasp such problems in his teeth and shake them until a clear answer emerged. He determined to hold the puzzle of ancestry in his mind; maybe someday he'd be able to solve it.

In the sargasso he had found not only danger but also friendship. Having someone to share the pleasures and the perils of life seemed quite important now. Being alone was the answer to very little. The direction in which he should travel became obvious to him: He must go home, to the cove.

10 · HOME AGAIN

Toward morning one moon later, Daniel reached Small Crab Island and climbed ashore. It had taken him a quarter-moon to find the edge of the continent and two more quarters to know whether home lay south or north. Now he was so close! He'd spent all his nights traveling and his days sleeping on small islands which bore few signs of bipeds. They might still be following him by means of the metal whiskers implanted on his shoulder. Twice he stayed on islands where he'd left treasures, and he made sure to leave some designs on the new stopping places. During his time on the floater and in the laboratory, he hadn't made any treasures; now, he did so with enjoyment and greater skill.

Daybreak came, and he passed into sleep. His dream raced on ahead: Would his brothers and sisters in the cove be glad to see him again? The dream woke him, and he decided to set off immediately for the cove.

In the midst of the sun-drenched morning, he entered the cove's encircling arms. Sea lions were lying on the rocks or swimming lazily in the tepid waters. There was Elbow Overhang—and the Whistler's Shelf—and the Singing Stones—and Bright Corner, where he'd cached his first collection of objects. Memories overwhelmed Daniel. He swam slowly about the perimeter of the cove, waiting for someone to recognize him. The familiar noises of the sea lions were wonderful to hear. Hagis the jokester, Achitopel the big eater, and others of his birth cohort were chatting and stretching, preparatory to their morning races. They were almost as large as Tashkent, who lay snoring on a high, choice ledge. It seemed to Daniel that virtually nothing had changed here since he'd gone away.

"Hello, fellas," he called to the bulls.

"Hello, yourself," Hagis said evenly, then turned back to address the others.

Perhaps the sun was in their eyes, Daniel thought, and they couldn't see him too well. He tried again. "I've been to the south," he said, "for quite a long time."

"Uh-huh," Hagis said, and continued talking to the others.

Daniel concealed his dismay at being treated like a stranger. It would give him time to look around and get the lay of the sand, before they figured out who he was.

"Going to race? I'm not a bad swimmer, myself," Daniel offered.

"Our races are closed to—"

"Where are your manners, Hagis?" Achitopel asked, a strand of kelp dangling from one tooth. "Care to join us, stranger?"

Daniel teamed with Achitopel to make the mindless runs to the north face of the cliff and back. He was careful not to win all the races nor to lose them all. In the breathing spells, he asked seemingly innocuous questions. Hagis and Achitopel, it turned out, were challenging Tashkent's leadership, figuring that two almost full-grown bulls, acting together, could best the old tyrant.

In the next series of races, Daniel tried one of his old maneuvers—something everyone in the tribe used to know that only he could do. But no one seemed to recognize it. He asked more questions and was amazed to learn that neither Hagis nor Achitopel had any memory of an adolescent sea lion once having lived here and having left the cove. It was as if he, Daniel, had never existed!

During the afternoon, Tashkent made two passes across Daniel's swim path, forcing him to veer off to avoid a collision. It was the old beachmaster's way of announcing his dominance. Frankly, Daniel didn't think the duo of Hagis and Achitopel would be able to make a successful challenge to the old bull.

Along with many other females, Anna came out to the observation ledges to get a good look at the stranger. She was still the most beautiful female of the tribe, and his heart skipped. She didn't stare frankly in his direction as others did. Had she, too, forgotten him? What had made them all lose their memories?

Leap tide began to pulse into the Singing Stones. Time for the ceremony. Daniel was surprised to see that Karl and the bipeds appeared, and were giving out food and wafers *before* the Singing, rather than after. In order not to be noticed by the bipeds, Daniel did not eat, and hid just inside a cave. Unfortunately, this put him at a distance from the ceremony.

Blossom and Esther led the Singing, and Daniel could see that the light-headedness induced by the wafers made them sing the verses much more lustily than of old. However, the songs rambled, and some were not said in the words he remembered from the era of Whistler Goshun. He himself ate neither the food nor the wafers, and sang the songs quietly. When the verses came to a close, play began, the sea lions not even waiting patiently for the sun to completely set. Angered at this gutting of the ceremony, Daniel slipped out of the cove, gazed at the sun until the ocean had swallowed it, then hunted. The cooler waters were bracing, and on the outer rim of the southern arm a bed of mussels and some rockfish enabled him to eat his fill within just a few moments. The food tasted delicious. Maybe, he thought, it was something in the cove's food that played tricks with memory. But day-old mackerel were still mackerel, weren't they? What about the wafers? They resembled no other sea lion food he'd ever had.

Returning inside, Daniel felt the warmer water and noted that the underwater fire-giving system had been turned on. All about, sea lions were pairing off for the night, singing songs of love.

The cove, he concluded, was a happy place; the bipeds, led by Karl, had done their job well here, and made of the place a haven of contentment for the tribe. But the water was so tepid and tame that no one had the energy to go out and hunt. Without the desire to brave cooler waters, without a knowledge of what had gone before, how could a sea lion ever be free?

He must return soon to the wider ocean. But first he had things to do here.

He went looking for Anna, only to discover that Tashkent had positioned himself squarely in front of her perch.

"She belongs to me," Tashkent growled.

"I don't belong to anyone," Anna said tartly. Daniel recalled that Hagis had mentioned that Anna was playing hard to get these days.

"Shut up, female," the old bull roared.

As if he hadn't heard Tashkent, Daniel smiled at Anna and climbed up to a slippery ledge. The leader leaped up and butted Daniel's flank, causing him to lose his hold and slip back into the water. Then he turned and readied a real assault. There was no way for Daniel to escape a fight.

The waters had grown dark. Daniel flipped over and raced for the north wall, picking up speed as he went. He got there a moment before Tashkent, made a sharp turn at just above bottom depth, and beat it for the south wall. Making certain that Tashkent was following at top speed, with his teeth only a dozen inches from Daniel's own flank, Daniel again evaded the big bull at the southern wall and sped for a new spot on the opposite wall. On this last transverse Daniel slowed a bit, as if he were tired, so that Tashkent was almost upon him and was gaining steadily. Daniel knew they were heading for the underwater observation glass which the bipeds used to watch the sea lions. In the dark, only the lead animal in this chase could adequately see it. Just as Daniel was approaching the glass he dove down, achieved a steep angle, and jumped out of the water onto a ledge. Tashkent, unable to see the wall in time, and going too fast to change direction, crashed his head into the glass.

Blood emerged from the old bull's mouth as he groaned and thrashed about in the water. Maybe a few teeth had been loosened. The dominant one would recover, and, Daniel knew, sooner or later he'd insist on a real fight to the death—but it wouldn't be tonight.

Swiftly Daniel reached the ledge near Anna. "Let's get acquainted," he said to her in a voice that allowed no refusals.

She looked at him with unwavering eyes. "What's your name, stranger?"

"Daniel. Daniel au Fond."

"That's a nice one."

It hurt that she no longer recognized him. Under the moonlight, they talked. "I heard you're playing hard to get," he said with a smile.

"Only for the bulls here," she said. "I'm waiting for a special someone."

"Long, dark, and handsome?"

"Maybe. Actually, I don't quite remember anymore. But I'll know him."

"How?"

"He once gave me something."

Daniel's heart skipped a beat. "A jewel, perhaps? A starfish with an agate center?"

Stunned into silence, Anna sat back on her haunches.

After a moment, she excused herself and went into the darkest part of a far cave. Daniel heard the faint sound of rocks being moved. She emerged with the jewel; the agate gleamed with the reflected light of the new moon.

Later, they mated.

"Daniel," she said. They embraced again.

The usual way for sea lions was to spend a night with a partner, then to reject the partner the next day and choose another. But the next day Daniel and Anna spent together, every moment of it, talking softly, swimming or sunning side by side. Not for a moment could they bear to be alone after having been separated for such a long time. He told her of his moons away from the cove, concealing nothing of the story, not even his time with Helen.

She spoke of her time of waiting, of how the bipeds in their sea-lion coverings had been entering the water more and more of late.

Tashkent stayed on a low ledge all day, hardly moving, watching everything, waiting, Daniel thought, for his opportunity to get revenge on the younger sea lion. Well, that would come when it came.

Daniel took care to hide again at the time of the Singing, when the bipeds were most in evidence. He would not let Anna eat the food or the wafers, wringing a promise from her to go hungry until he returned with food for them both.

Outside on the southern rim, he hunted more quickly and efficiently than ever, so she would not have long to wait. They ate together. Daniel noticed that Tashkent took no food nor wafers this night, either. It concerned him.

By the following morning, the light in Anna's eyes was clearer. She began to remember more events and times—some of which she wished would have stayed forgotten, such as rough treatment from Tashkent. Daniel was happy at the return of her memory, and decided that it was the wafers that had made her lose it in the first place. It couldn't have been the food fish, because in the laboratory and on the floater he'd been fed the same kind of dead fish, and hadn't forgotten anything.

That afternoon, as they were embracing, Anna laughed and said, "I've got it—the secret I was going to tell you long ago."

Daniel groaned. "How can you joke at a moment like this?"

"I had a secret from our last time together; I didn't tell it to you then, because I was annoyed at you. So . . ."

"Well, what was it?"

"Daniel, I'm carrying a pup."

This time it was Daniel who was stunned. He nuzzled her and said it was the best news he'd had since returning.

"And why," she asked, her eyes full of merriment, "why did you come home?"

"You," he answered, "you are home."

11 · THE NEW BEGINNING

~~~~~~

Near noon on his third day back at the cove, Daniel spotted the familiar shape of Fred the trainer on the escarpment. The biped was searching about, but hadn't yet fixed his gaze on Daniel, who was on a far ledge next to Anna. He didn't say much to Anna about sighting Fred, but she sensed his uneasiness, and he had to explain.

"For a biped, he's not bad."

"What do you mean, 'not bad'?"

Bipeds had saved their lives. Bipeds, Daniel had to admit, were friendly—quite so, in the case of Fred—and yet Daniel's feelings about them were mixed. He pointed out to Anna that they must have traced him here through the metal whiskers in his shoulder.

"He's after me, and if I—if we—were to leave, Fred could follow us by following the signals."

"We might as well stay, then."

Staying was an idea: A pup could be raised more easily within the cove's protecting arms than out on the ocean. On the other flipper, how could they prevent the pup from eating the wafers? For that matter, why had no pups been born into the cove, if it was such a wonderful place?

Anna thought it might have something to do with the wafers. Perhaps they also prevented the females from carrying pups to birth. They discussed the possibility for a while. Actually, they were talking about everything. It was as if Anna had just been waiting to speak. She had many intriguing notions. For instance, she believed that the older sea lions didn't wish to leave the cove because they'd been so deeply scarred mentally by the typhoon. What they longed for was security and protection. It was for just such observations that Daniel had always loved Anna.

As they chatted, from the corners of their eyes they watched Fred, who never left the escarpment but who also did not make any move toward recapturing Daniel.

The sun dropped lower in the sky, the rocks began to hum, and it was time for the Singing. So as not to be conspicuous by their absence, Daniel and Anna moved near the Singing Stones. It irked Daniel to see the lumbering Blossom atop Bright Corner, leading the ceremony. His anger carried through the first part of the verses, and he wasn't listening too carefully until it came time for the lines about Beachmaster Saul. He heard the two old females sing:

> *"Deep, the realm of Beachmaster Saul,*
> *Where the creatures great and small*
> *Made attack upon sea lions all,*
> *And drove us to our cove, our home,*
> *From which we never seek to roam . . ."*

Daniel couldn't believe what he was hearing. This was not the verse seared into his soul, the clarion call to the lions that lived in the sea to "travel far in mystery."

"That's not how it goes," he whispered to Anna.

Several of the sea lions hissed at them. "Stranger, be quiet," Esther warned. "Maybe in your territory they do things differently, but here we sing it this way. Always have."

"Not in the time of Grandfather Goshun."

Across the way, Tashkent's massive head lifted, and gazed in his direction. Daniel shut up suddenly as Anna butted him in the ribs. Daniel was silent, but waves of anger battered his resolve to be still.

Nightfall did not calm him down. Whenever one of the older females passed him, Daniel glowered. Anna had to practically order him to accompany her to Grunting Cave. Once there, however, he forgot about everything except her.

The next morning they did a few laps about the cove, trawling near the surface, and hardly noticed when no one nodded good morning to them. But when Daniel directly greeted the chunky food-lover Achitopel, and his brother swam by him as if he weren't there, Anna shivered and they both pulled up on a ledge.

"They've been told to ignore us, to treat us as if we didn't exist," she whispered to Daniel.

"That's ridiculous," Daniel snapped.

But it was true.

When Daniel tried to take part in the morning's races, jokester Hagis looked straight through him, formed teams of everyone else, and raced without him. Anna went to the flat perch where the females mutually groomed one another; Blossom, Esther, and the others all moved away, not everyone at once, but casually, as if Anna weren't there. Blossom was the last one to leave, and Anna blocked her way off a perch, asking hoarsely, "Why are you doing this to us? We haven't harmed anyone."

"Did you hear a sea gull?" Blossom said to Esther. "Can't quite make out what it's saying."

"Didn't hear nothing," Esther laughed, and dove into a breaking wave, knocking Anna from her perch as if by accident.

Anna swam to Daniel, shook herself free of excess water, and frowned. "I don't like it. They're trying to ignore us to death."

"That can't be done unless we cooperate. Don't take it lying down, love. We might as well have some fun out of it."

To demonstrate, Daniel swam into the midst of a speed lane, and lolled there. Achitopel had to maneuver around him, and, in so doing, lost a race. But since he was supposed to be ignoring Daniel, he couldn't very well chew him out for spoiling a victory. Achitopel looked cross. Anna giggled. Her courage returned.

The lovers went about making it evident to the tribe what a foolish endeavor the old females had begun. In a sense, being ignored gave to Daniel and Anna permission to be obnoxious. Anna teased Hagis about his bad jokes and Achitopel about his obesity. Daniel told Esther precisely what had happened to her once-legendary good looks. After a half-tide, this teasing was no longer fun, and so they began to tell the tribe, more seriously, things that they hoped would hurt or at least provoke reactions. At the tops of their voices they both shouted that the sea lions in the cove were slaves to the wishes of the bipeds. That the creatures who cleaned the metal worms off the bottom and fed the sea lions were the same ones who kept pups from being born. That the proffered food and wafers destroyed sea lions' initiative and memory.

By day's end, both were hoarse, and knew full well that their shouting had not changed the minds of any sea lions in the tribe.

"We're going to have to leave, after all, Anna. Even if the bipeds follow us."

"You're right. We have no choice. But when?"

"Now."

They were on the far ledge, watching the tribe eat the food and wafers and do their botched Singing. They looked at one another, and slipped together down the rocks and into the water. However, as they headed toward the cove's mouth, they found their way blocked.

In what was obviously a prearranged movement, Hagis, Achitopel, and some of the other bulls swam around Anna and isolated her from Daniel. There were too many of them for him to best at once. The bulls moved Anna away, and Tashkent swam in front of Daniel and looked him in the eye. As the younger bulls nudged Anna over to a ledge on the northern arm and stood guard about her, the rest of the tribe, forsaking the Singing, scrambled onto ledges and waited for the fight between the beachmaster and the blasphemer.

Daniel knew that if he and Anna were to be able to depart from the cove, he would have to defeat Tashkent thoroughly, once and for all. He also believed that only one bull would survive this fight.

With that, he rushed the old bull with the nails on his foreflippers and raked open the wound on Tashkent's nose. But one blow was not the whole fight. When Daniel bore in for another, Tashkent was ready, and cut a similar swath across Daniel's cheek. The water in front of Daniel's eyes reddened. He recalled how each evening blood from the dying sun would spill onto the ocean, and let the legend inspire him: The sun's wound, which dated from the time of Saul, was the sign of a hurt that caused not death, but rebirth. Like the sun, Daniel would rise again!

For what seemed like forever they fought in the water, exchanging blows, flipper rakes, sharp bites. Tashkent was slightly larger, but Daniel, who knew that his entire future depended on victory, had the strength of ten. He would not give in.

It was past dark when they clambered onto the ledge above the Singing Stones—Daniel could reach it now, even in midtide. He felt it was right and fitting to fight here, with his haunches set in the tide pools, defending Bright Corner. This place was as much his as any in the cove could be.

With a scream, Tashkent leaped forward and landed on Daniel's head and shoulders. The big bull dug in with his teeth. Pain seared Daniel. Something ripped with an awful sound. As Daniel twisted his body to get away from the terrible teeth, he saw Tashkent pause to spit out some flesh—and metal.

"So much for magic, Daniel!" the bull roared, his mouth red with blood and gore.

In a daze, Daniel realized that Tashkent must have thought the device in Daniel's shoulder had something to do with his "strange" behavior. No matter! The signal sender was out. And Tashkent had remembered his name!

For a moment Daniel felt weak. Tashkent stood over him, poised for further vengeance, but not taking it. Why? "Do you yield?" the bull roared. Then, more quietly, said: "Stay, and in time it will all be yours."

A surge of power shot through Daniel. Ignoring the hurt in his shoulder, he squirmed from under Tashkent, turned, and rushed the beachmaster, then butted him for all he was worth. Tashkent seemed surprised. Again and again Daniel lunged with his head, until the great bull lost his footing and fell, crashing into the cleft in the rocks that were the Singing Stones. There the leader's body lay, wedged between two immense stones. With a bloodlust he hadn't known he possessed, Daniel sprang down on top of Tashkent, pushing him farther into the cleft. Tashkent was alive, but unable to move. Daniel raised his teeth above his adversary's throat.

One part of him wanted to destroy Tashkent. But another told him it was not necessary—and, besides, the old bull might be his father. Daniel stood heaving over the leader and stared into his dazed eyes.

"We're going, old one," Daniel said firmly. "Remember that I could have killed you and didn't." In his heart, Daniel knew that Tashkent could say the same thing: At his moment of victory, Tashkent had pulled back from Daniel's throat.

Daniel moved himself off the leader, whose body remained pinned into the stones. Daniel swam slowly over to where Hagis, Achitopel, and the other young adult bulls guarded Anna. None of the males would challenge him.

guarded Anna. None of the males would challenge him. They moved aside, and, with a cry, Anna joined Daniel in midcove.

The crescent moon spread patches of invitation on the dark blue beyond as Daniel and Anna swam out of the cove's mouth and into the cold waters of freedom.

Part Three

~~~~~~

TOGETHER

12 · TOGETHER

*H*uddled together on the outer rocks of the cove's southern arm, the lovers were only a few lengths from their former home, yet were completely separate from everything Anna had always known. For fear of sharks that might be attracted by his seeping blood, Daniel had insisted they spend their first night out of the cove on solid ground. Anna shivered until sleep came. Daniel closed his eyes but did not rest. His wounds throbbed. Each pulse beat reminded him of the battle. Had Tashkent let him up because he knew that Daniel was his son? He couldn't resolve the matter.

At dawn they headed west, to Small Crab Island. Because Daniel's wounds were unhealed and his body was sore, they traveled slowly. The unhurried pace enabled Daniel to talk Anna through her first exposure to cold waters, and the need to be continually alert for sharks and biped floaters with whirlers that could cut a sea lion in half.

Small Crab Island was, as he'd remembered it, a hard, joyless place with no comforts. The cairn of stones he had so carefully shaped during his first visit was still mostly intact, though a few pieces had been blown down by storms. While Anna excitedly nosed about the rocks, he repaired the damage to his design. Anna disturbed the gulls and sent the crabs scurrying as she leaped from rock to rock, exploring the meager confines of the island. Her zest allowed Daniel to put his aches and exhaustion out of mind.

Next dawn, when she saw the sun rise out of the sea, she was as astounded as he had been, and he chuckled at her amazement. That day they hunted together. Near the bottom, Anna's more compact body allowed her greater maneuverability among the stones and corals. They evolved a plan: Daniel would wait, just out of a bottom fish's sight, and Anna would flush the fish toward him so he could catch it. In this manner they easily captured several flounder and had enough food for a whole day.

The days and nights were full. They practiced hunting, endurance swims, power dives. She built tolerance for the cold. His mane grew and his left shoulder healed, though it would never have the mobility it had shown when he was younger. She became leaner, more muscular. He learned something about patience in his role as striker to her chaser. They had a lot to discover about each other. Were they at their best in the mornings, or after dark? Did they have to chat all the time, or could they exist together in silence without feeling the need to talk? By the time a moon had shed her coat and come out again, they were very close.

Unable to properly identify a ratfish, they were sick for two days. Anna ran herself up on the spine of a blowfish, and suffered until it worked its way through the flesh of her cheek. Several storms battered them: During one, they lost their bearings and were parted for an hour. The reunion was so full of warmth it almost made up for the agony of separation. They had a spat. They made up. After a week, Daniel ceased searching the horizon each dawn for signs of bipeds. There were none.

Daniel wondered how he'd ever managed to exist without a mate. Under the impetus of showing Anna the ocean world, his own understanding grew. On his previous journey, he had seldom taken the time to go to the bottom, hover there, and watch the mesmerizing show. Now they lay on the bottom together, just far enough down for the sun to cast dappled coral shadows on the sands. Lying like this one afternoon, they came across a litter of infant octopuses whose antics provided laughs for them both. Later, Anna fashioned a dance mimicking the creatures. She said it would remind them of this time and this place and this feeling they had that the world was theirs to explore.

Anna now realized, she told Daniel, how unhappy she'd been in the cove—even though, for most of the time she lived there, she'd never thought of it.

"If you had dragged me out with you when you left with Goshun's body, I might not have stayed with you."

"You weren't ready for freedom then, and I wasn't ready for a real mate."

Later, Daniel teased her: "What would you have done if I'd never come back?"

"Maybe become like Blossom, sour to everyone."

"Sour? Not you."

"Why not? Besides, I think she may have been my mother. One can't be sure. She's never been very warm to me."

"Or to anyone, it seems."

They talked of the track of the sun across a cloud-filled

sky, the water temperature at various depths, the way winds roiled the bottom sands for days after a storm's passage, the incredible variety of creatures in the ocean. Anna felt life stirring in her abdomen, and said she thought it was the cooler waters of the past moon that had started the pup growing. Maybe it had been the warm bath of the cove, rather than the wafers, that inhibited the growth process. Maybe many of the females there were pregnant, but would never live in conditions that would encourage their pups to be born.

Mention of the pup brought a burst of feeling to Daniel. He recited for her, with a faraway look in his eye, every verse and notion about the legend of Beachmaster Saul, the thirteen tribes, the insistence that the true lions of the sea had sprung from Pacifica. This new pup, he vowed, would be the inheritor of a grand lineage.

"You know, Daniel, that whole story is full of rubbish."

"What?"

"A silly male legend. There wouldn't be any sea lions without the Great Mother, Selchie. Other than her, though, there's hardly a mention of a cow anywhere in the story. All bulls. How ridiculous!"

"Well, er, uh, I think, ah—"

"How do you suppose all those tribes were born and brought up, Daniel? Without females, your fabled race of lions of the sea wouldn't exist!"

He had to admit that she was correct. And while she had him on the defensive, she told him of the old cows' tale that pups were supposed to be born in the region of ice. This struck a chord in him, but he teased her: "Are you sure that's not just another story that has no basis in fact?"

"I feel it in my bones, Daniel—the cold is necessary to the start of sea-lion life. Anyway, we ought to go there; it's something we have to do."

"It will be a long journey to the north."

"Can we start tomorrow morning, then?"

"Well, I hadn't planned—"

"Oh, thank you! I knew you'd understand." She nuzzled him, and that was that.

13 · COUSINS

*L*eaving the little hump of rocks behind them, Daniel and Anna set out the next morning. They followed the North Star.

Eager for the journey, they nevertheless shared a pang of regret at quitting Small Crab Island, where they had been so carefree and isolated together. They flew through the water at a steady pace, with harmonized thrusts of their foreflippers. After a while, they knew each other's movement patterns, and when Daniel veered slightly left, right, or down to avoid a swell or floating obstacle, Anna matched his actions, so that they remained in tandem. By late afternoon the lovers were thousands of lengths away from their starting point, just out of sight of land, and swept along in the rhythmic beat of their bodies against the ocean.

For another moon, they kept on pushing north. Day after day they swam, holding the coast in view or just out of sight, beyond the green-blue horizon. During the nights, they slept on small islands or sometimes took short naps at sea. They felt the urgency of the pup's approach. Each day was colder than the one before. After a quarter-moon, they spotted the first of the ice floes. A few days later, they swam among floating ice chunks all the time. By the end of the half-moon, they were disconcerted to

note that the sun only rose above the horizon for part of the day before plunging back into the sea. If they swam too far, would the sun cease to rise altogether?

Anna felt birth pains. They began to search in the immediate vicinity for a place on which to bring the pup into the world. Anna had a definite image in mind: an island or protected inlet where there was soft grass and not too many rocks to spoil the approach to the beach. Daniel argued for a site more remote and rocky, so enemies couldn't approach, but she convinced him that a young pup, while learning to survive, would not necessarily be able to scramble up rocks and onto high perches to escape heavy seas. He didn't protest much—after all, it was she who was carrying the pup.

Next day they found the perfect spot, an exposed but pretty island several thousand lengths from the coastline. Shaped like a bird, it consisted of a "body" of five acres where the tundra grass covered nubbly rock outcroppings, and a long "neck" of boulders that curved off into the sea at an angle that deflected powerful waves from breaking over the beach of the "body." When the wind blew the grass, it seemed almost as if the bird's feathers were ruffling in flight.

The site had much to recommend it—not the least that it was already inhabited by a colony of seals, who, though complete strangers, looked enough like descendants of Saul to be cousins.

Daniel encountered the adult males immediately on approaching through the surf. Their territories extended from the beach many yards into the ocean, and they patrolled underwater with barks and cries, occasionally striking at one another in their vehemence. The seals had fur, but no sagittal crests, such as he now bore. Dappled, gray, and round, the adults' shapes reminded him of the cigars Sigmund smoked.

He told Anna to go on ahead to shore, and he prepared to confront one of the seals for a piece of territory. Although there were many cries and growls, it was no contest—Daniel was far larger, and the seal had to give way. He rode a breaker past the dappled seal to the beach, and was astounded to see dozens and dozens of the dappled females and as many newborn pups. The beauty of the pups was wonderful to behold. Covered with soft white fur which set off their large, coal-black eyes, they seemed, Daniel said to Anna, almost like clouds scurrying across the sky on a day of high winds.

"Or like small ice floes," she answered. The small ones appeared to melt into the thin patches of snow still visible on parts of the island.

At the mention of the ice floes, Daniel's heart leaped. Here was another fragment from the legend come to life. It was real, and right in front of him, not just some old story!

Cows were giving birth everywhere. They seemed to need the open beach and flat land for the purpose—a rocky surface would have been wrong. "Baby come soon?" a nursing female asked, her voice low and rich. Anna responded, and a conversation started. The cousin named herself as Parduk. She said that she was one of the cows of the old, wiry-looking bull on a ridge, whose name was Lokat; he was, she said, the beachmaster.

Beachmaster! In this setting, the title made more sense:

He was the bull who controlled the greatest amount of territory. Lokat stayed on the highest point of the island, a clump of rocks overlooking the beach, and would let no other males near his harem. On a far corner of the island that was more covered with stones and pebbles than beach, a dozen adolescent males fought—grunting, roaring, and lunging at one another.

"No mind boys on hauling ground," Lokat said to Daniel. "They hurt none." He laughed and looked Daniel up and down, gauging the difference in size and power between himself and the interloper. Daniel made no move to rut with the females that seemed to be edging into his own corner of the beach, so Lokat had no reason to begin a fight. The beachmaster snorted and raised his head in a proud way, indicating his harem. "Meeyon," he said, pointing at an especially attractive younger female whose eyes were masked by a dark patch of skin.

The day drew quickly to a close. Before Daniel was ready for it, the sun went down. All about, the cousins were moving together for kamarla, and a few were eating food. Daniel wondered what they were smashing with rocks held in flippers, and was introduced to a new food, the long-legged crabs of these chilly waters. He found them meaty, if difficult to eat.

Shortly after moonrise, the dappled ones began a cere-mony. The already sleepy pups were massed together in the island's center, ringed by the females and then by the males. Elders such as Lokat and Parduk took perches on the few rocks. Another elder, Vaz, who had only one functioning eye, lifted his head to the stars and began a low chant. The tribe did the same, their heads aimed at a group of light points quite near the North Star; they addressed this constellation as none other than the Great Beachmaster, Saul.

Daniel looked at the starry outline, and felt very dumb.

Clearly visible, Beachmaster Saul sat comfortably in the sky, flippers stretched in front of his body. How could a sea lion never have seen Saul in the stars before? There was so much Daniel had to learn.

> *"Oh, Great Saul, save us all!*
> *Beachmaster, Beachmaster,*
> *Heed our call.*
> *Forgive us if we have done wrong;*
> *Save us, save us, be mighty and strong!"*

Daniel found the cousins' chant odd. In their singing, Saul was addressed as a remote and fearsome figure whose benevolence and help had to be courted with food and other offerings. The furry seals begged Saul to bestow on them the strength to endure the difficulties of their lives. There were no adventures of Saul mentioned, much less celebrated. They just asked this powerful ancestor to "save" them from something. While the parents chanted, the beautiful white pups hummed along; as yet, they could follow neither the words nor the tune of the singing.

One part of the ceremony ended, but others seemed to begin. As mothers and pups called to one another through the darkness, the males hauled fish, mussels, and crabs to leave, uneaten, on the high rocks. By the time this was done, the pups had fallen asleep, and the males joined the females in kamarla. Anna and Daniel also came to huddle together, and experienced the shared warmth against the chill of the night, the feeling of extended family, the over-lapping and interlocking of bodies. In a way they had never felt in their home cove, they became part of this tribe. Kamarla, too, was more understandable in this setting.

Morning was a long time in arriving, and, in the extended period of grayness that preceded the sun's lifting above the horizon, Anna had sharp pains. She told Daniel to go take a long swim, and not to be too quick about returning to the island.

A bit hurt by her bluntness, Daniel nevertheless did as he was bidden. Swimming away from the island, dodging ice floes, he noticed that a pack of sea gulls was pecking away at the food which the colony had left as an offering to Beachmaster Saul. Well, he reasoned, birds did come out of the sky, which was, or so the cousins believed, the home cove of the ancient Beachmaster.

The sun had reached halfway up in the sky. In terms of these northern waters, that was as far up as it got during the day. Daniel chose this moment to return, and loped out of the cold, viscous waters across the beach and to the clump of grass where Anna lay on her side. She was licking a small sleeping bundle that was cuddled next to her. It was a male.

"He's so small," Daniel said, amazed. Anna nodded weakly and kept licking the fur, smoothing it with her tongue. Daniel examined the creature from all angles, taking delight in the perfection of all his miniature features. His fur was the color of wet sand.

Much to the amusement of the cousins, whose pups were left alone except for suckling and ceremony times,

Anna and Daniel spent all day with their little one, watching as he rose on uncertain flippers and moved about. He reached the ocean, and several unwanted mouthfuls of water slid into his belly before he thought to paddle with his lips closed.

The pup, Daniel thought, was quite helpless, beautifully small, and very much the product of himself and the tired, smiling Anna. A fierce protectiveness rose in him: Never would he allow harm to come either to his female or to his firstborn. So long as he had strength, Daniel would obtain food for them both, find a place where storms would not tear the little one away from his mother, fight invaders to the death—he would do anything to assure the small inheritor of his blood the chance for life. Suddenly the rightful name for the pup appeared in his mind.

"We'll call him Goshun," Daniel told Anna. She kissed them both. But when they tried to tell the cousins of the pup's name, the dappled ones grew alarmed.

"No name now," Parduk cautioned. The other females shook their heads and made sharp clucking sounds. "No pups has name, now. Maybe in summer—if Saul smile."

Daniel and Anna glanced at each other, as if to share the thought: But what if the Beachmaster in the Sky did *not* smile?

14 · NIGHTMARE

*E*very day Goshun did something new—floated suc-
cessfully, ate a piece of solid food, made a good hunting motion, said a word properly—and several moon
quarters passed quickly. Anna's milk was rich, and he grew
steadily, as did the other pups around them. The seals'
pups, however, had more difficulty in swimming, and
couldn't yet float without assistance.

The weather changed. Each succeeding day the sun rose
earlier, set later, and seemed to give off more warmth. The
summer days, Parduk told them dreamily, were so wonderful that it was hard to wait. Small purple flowers pushed
through the tundra grass; Daniel tried to eat one, but it
was protected by a burr at the base of the petals. Meeyon
giggled at Daniel's ignorance and spent some time teaching
him about the foliage of these harsh islands—the blue lu-
pine, red and purple fernleafs, primrose, forget-me-not,
the pink moss campion. When they were isolated from the
tribe, Meeyon made a mating posture, and Daniel covered
her. Later, he understood that Lokat had done the same
with Anna. It was part of becoming members of the tribe.
Daniel and Anna still spent the nights together.

Ice floes continued to drift by on the currents; as the
melting chunks became smaller and less frequent sights,
the white pups which so resembled the floes stood out

more brightly against the grass and the sea. Birds flew over, and Daniel learned about these as well—he'd never seen them before: longspur, snow bunting, sandpiper, rosy finch.

Despite the prohibition against calling the cousins' pups by name, Daniel and Anna came to know many of the little white ones—this seal had extra-large flippers, another showed a discoloration on the forehead, a third was unusually perky. The sea lions nuzzled, wrestled, and raced the white pups as they did with their own. Goshun mimicked the fierce growls of the adolescent males of the hauling ground; in one so young, the pose was endearing. Daniel was partial to Goshun, but Anna was impossible with him, feeding him her milk at all tides, spending time grooming him, letting him sleep underneath her flipper to receive added warmth during the still-chilly nights.

Quite early on a dark, fogbound morning, Daniel came out of the water with a fat salmon in his mouth.

"You go Anna?" Lokat asked from the high rock. When Daniel nodded, Lokat responded that he hardly had time to eat these days, so busy was he enforcing his territory and exhausting himself with all the females. Of course Meeyon was an especial favorite, but he had to service them all.

"You need your strength, then," Daniel observed, and flipped him the salmon, which Lokat greedily downed. Daniel appreciated the wiry leader's charm; besides, it was the season for the salmon, and it took little effort to capture them. Suddenly, Lokat's head jerked up, and he stared beyond the females down on the beach, in the direction of the coast. Daniel followed his gaze, and in a short while saw things coming through the mists.

"Floaters," Daniel said. Lokat nodded but could voice nothing, the words apparently stuck in his throat.

At last Lokat muttered, "O great Saul, save us all," and turned his eyes away from Daniel.

As the mists cleared, from the highest point on the island Daniel could make out three floaters with bipeds in them. The floaters' approach had been muffled and concealed by the fog. The wooden, narrow things were rough-edged and rode high in the water, powered by whirlers. Ten bipeds, all shorter and darker-skinned than those he remembered, were covered in cloths the color of the murky sea. A few yards from shore, the bipeds jumped out of the floaters and drew them onto the beach.

Then they took some large sticks out of the floaters, and walked deliberately to points on the perimeter of the island. They seemed to know precisely what they were about, and where they were going; the cousins' barked challenges did not deter them. In a moment, the bipeds stood on the island's edges, wooden sticks on their shoulders, waiting.

Parduk, Meeyon, and the other mothers on the tundra called to their pups. Lokat and Vaz stared up to where the stars of Beachmaster Saul had appeared last night, and chanted. Daniel believed in the great sea lion in the sky, but this was no time for verses!

"Anna," he shouted, "take Goshun off the island."

"Why should we do—?"

"Don't argue. These bipeds show no love in their eyes."

From the high rock he saw with relief that Anna was

using her brain. Goshun wanted to peek at what was going on, but she wouldn't let him. As he protested all the way, Anna pushed and coaxed him to the southern edge of the island, where small rocks and a beach of jagged gravel usually kept seals and sea lions away. Only one biped stood guard there. Anna avoided him, and bumped the squealing, tan-coated Goshun off the tundra and onto the gravel. The pup howled that the stones hurt the soles of his flippers; Anna brooked no nonsense, and shoved him out among the waves. The biped did not stop them. Mother and pup swam for the point on the horizon where gray clouds merged with the surface of the sea.

Daniel wanted to join them, but knew he must stay and fight, or at least witness what was about to happen.

A biped raised a broad stick and brought it down with force on the head of one of the young white pups. The terrible sound of bones cracking traveled through the air, and the pup collapsed on the grass and ceased to move; a trickle of blood seeped from his skull.

It happened so quickly! The pup died before Daniel's scream could get out of his mouth. Another raised stick. Another smash. Another body fell to the grass. Daniel could see the life go out of the pup's eyes the moment the stick crushed its skull.

When Daniel found his voice, his scream was joined by those of the cousins and their frightened little ones. The bipeds were all around, raising up their broad sticks and swinging them down on the heads of the nameless, white-furred pups. The killers walked with purposeful strides, rhythmically stroking their instruments of death through the air as they roamed the grass, the beach, the meager rocks. The smell of blood was heavy in the nostrils. Here and there, some of the cousins tried to attack, rushing the bipeds and biting them. Among these brave seals was the old cow, Parduk. For her pains a stick was slung low, and bashed in her side. She limped away.

Daniel resisted the impulse to attack. It would be senseless to die in a rush at such an overwhelmingly powerful fighter, especially since his family was out of harm's way. He kept to the high ground, prepared to leap off, if necessary. But why did no biped attack him? And why, when the older seals lunged to get off the island, did the killers let them pass? Near the spot where Anna had pushed off with Goshun, Meeyon herded her own pup—the one with the slight discoloration—and, in company of several adolescent bulls, two other young ones. All leaped together onto the sharp gravel, virtually upending one biped. Seeing the opening, three more pups rushed toward freedom. The biped recovered his feet and was about to follow them into the waves, but another called him back to the killing.

Daniel's mind reeled. Why this slaughter? If the cousins had known that it might occur, why hadn't they fled earlier to another island or to a spot on the coast? Why were only the young being killed?

After a while, no more sticks were raised. The bipeds dragged the bodies of the clubbed pups toward the sandy beach and the floaters. Some of the white youngsters still writhed, their muscles jerking even after the life had gone from their eyes. Blood was everywhere. It stained their fur, the grass, the sticks.

Near the floaters, the other bipeds attacked the dead and dying pups with silver teeth held in their hands. Swift strokes cut and pulled at the fur until each pelt came off in a single, ugly piece. Daniel was sickened at the noise of skin being ripped from the pups' bodies, the sight of denuded muscles, of internal organs scattered on the ground. He spewed out his entire previous day's food. The stench mingled with the blood that suffused the air. He screamed at the bipeds to stop—even made the flipper sign for it that he had practiced with trainer Fred—but these bipeds just kept stripping the bodies, piling dozens of the skins in the floaters. At last Daniel understood: The pups were being slaughtered because of their beautiful white fur.

Death covered the island like an inescapable dense fog. Everywhere he looked—and he could not shut his eyes—biped arms were aloft, slashing with their silver teeth. A thousand biped arms. "Mandragar," he whispered to himself. Here, indeed, was sealiondom's ultimate enemy.

~~~~~

After some time—how long, exactly, he did not know—the floaters left. They rode lower in the water, loaded with bloodstained skins. The sun, now clear of clouds, threw unshadowed, cruel light on the carcasses of the fallen pups. Birds circled, waiting impatiently for the seals to leave them the carrion. When Anna and Goshun clambered back onshore, Daniel greeted them with a dull bark.

Daniel put a flipper out to Goshun and cried. Anna's eyes, too, were full. The youngster peered quizzically at them both, as if unable to understand what was upsetting them.

Later, Meeyon and the bulls returned, but with only a single pup—her own, slightly discolored one. The others had drowned because the adult seals could not hold them up long enough in the water. Sharks had them now.

So great were the hurts of their friends and distant relatives that Daniel and Anna could take no comfort in their own pup's survival. Lokat, Vaz, the injured Parduk, and the other dappled cousins wandered among the dead, their voices rent by loss. Because the skins had been ripped from the bodies, individual pups could not even be identified by the grieving parents.

Anna whispered to Daniel: "The cousins refused to name their pups because they didn't want to become too attached to those destined for slaughter."

The dozen surviving pups, fear in their eyes, were formed up close behind Lokat. Vaz brought up their rear as the tribe loped to a spot where there were no bodies. Daniel looked at the surviving ones closely—Goshun was dark, Meeyon's pup was discolored. Among the missing were the one with the large flippers and the perky little male. Another survivor had taken a blow that missed the central part of his skull but mashed an eye. In time, Vaz said, he would take this pup as his assistant.

Lokat's gaze, which had avoided Daniel's in the moment before the disaster, sought it now.

"As they be older, they forget. They be happy they not die."

Daniel lowered his head. He thought, but did not say: No, they'll not forget. And neither would Daniel au Fond.

15 · THE TASK

~~~~~~~~~~~~~~~~~~~~~~~~~~~~~~

*S*hortly after the disaster, Lokat led the tribe from the island of birth and death to a small, rocky coastal inlet remarkable for the great abundance of fish and crabs nearby.

It was midsummer before Daniel's memory of the slaughter began to subside so he could again pay attention to the world around him. He was puzzled that most of the cousins did not grieve for the murdered pups as he and Anna did; the only real sufferer among them was Parduk, who could not remember a cycle of moons in which any son or daughter of hers had survived. The glorious weather and the serenity of the resting place seemed cruel. But even Daniel had to admit that it was hard to mourn when all about the seas and land was beautiful and full of life. The weather was warm, the salmon were running, the big crabs were especially flavorful. Flies were the only annoyance: Almost as large as small birds, they pierced the skin with their bites.

The cousins' pups lost their white birth coats and rapidly developed the dappled appearance of their parents. They also were given names.

One night the sky hardly darkened, and the cousins began to scurry about, gathering kelva berries. These had emerged, Daniel was told, two moons ago during a short-lived warm spell, then had frozen again on their vines. Now they were edible, but, more than that, Vaz explained, ingesting them would induce a dreamlike state— if the eating occurred during the proper ceremony. The next evening, though the sky blackened slightly for a time, there was really no night; a few moments after sunset, the red- and green-tinged clouds of dawn could be seen. The only things that weren't visible in the sky were the constellations, including that of Beachmaster Saul. To Daniel, this seemed fitting.

That night, under the influence of the berries, Vaz led the singers in song after song, appealing to Beachmaster Saul to come back to them, to bring back real night. Dancing and singing continued until all the cousins were exhausted, and beyond. Honor would come to the first tribal member to announce correctly the moment of the reappearance of the constellation.

Little Goshun ate two berries and promptly fell asleep, as did the other youngsters who indulged. Daniel and Anna ate a few, and felt light-headed, but didn't join in the ceremony. However, giddy with the berries, Daniel could no longer control his anger.

"Why are they asking Saul for help?" he asked Anna. "The Great Beachmaster did nothing to protect the tribe or to prevent the killing of the pups."

"Not so loud, Daniel."

"Isn't it the truth?"

"Unfortunately, yes," she said quietly.

"Did the cousins do anything wrong, either in their ceremonies that we saw, or in the way they were living? Was it anything that *we* did? Can the disaster be blamed on allowing us to stay with them?"

"No, none of that. The killing is just something that . . . happens. Every cycle, apparently, from what Parduk told me."

"Then why appeal for Saul's return?"

Neither had an answer. Both wondered about the wisdom of asking help from the stars. It was one thing to sing in joy to the setting sun and to recite old tales of adventure; it was quite another to assume that control over one's life was in the flippers of some great, unknowable entity in the sky whose appearance could not even be counted on.

During the period when Saul was gone from the sky, three odd events occurred.

Meeyon, Lokat's favorite cow, openly sought Daniel's protection and coupled with him in sight of Lokat. She soon became a second mate for Daniel.

Goshun, waking after his sleep on the wings of the berries, began to cry uncontrollably. "The pups, the pups," he sobbed, and pleaded with Daniel to tell him it was a bad dream. This Daniel refused to do. Certain realities, he counseled both Goshun and Anna, had to be accepted because rejecting them would not make them go away.

The third event was the appearance of a pair of bipeds on the high rocks that overlooked the inlet. Daniel saw them and raised the alarm. Lokat, though dazed by berries, informed Daniel calmly that bipeds wouldn't harm seals at this time of the cycle; in fact, he pointed out, the bipeds were singing in the colony's direction—appealing to the stars, as it were, just as the seals did. Daniel was unwilling to accept the intruders' benevolence. He hurried Anna and the sleepy Goshun out to sea for an entire day. When they returned, the hunters had gone but the seals' celebration was still going strong. Moments later Voola, apprentice of Vaz, called out that he could see the Beachmaster's "eye," which was the brightest star in the sky, the only one to succeed in piercing the twilight.

In the following few moons, as the night reappeared and the arc of the sun drooped lower and lower, biped hunters showed up several times, but did nothing more than sing in the tribe's honor. Vaz told Daniel that as far back as any seal could remember, there had been hunters—and that, in the spring, the hunters had pursued the tribe and taken pups from them. So: There were "eternal hunters" in the "region of ice." Daniel took some satisfaction in this new evidence of the truth behind the old legends passed on to him from his dying grandfather's lips.

"What you talk about, Dan'l?"

"Nothing, little Goshun."

"Is not nothin'."

Goshun was right, of course, and Daniel decided it was time to tell him, in plain words, about the hunters and then about his great-grandfather and the start of Daniel's journeys. The pup's eyes widened and he nodded his head—but how much did he really understand? Daniel couldn't be sure.

The cousins' implied acceptance of the inevitability of the hunters' attacks upset Daniel. The slaughter on Bird's Neck had convinced him, at least, that bipeds could no longer be considered his friends. During his life there had been bipeds who were kind to him—Karl and Fred, principally—but, on balance, the sons of Kanonah were the only living beings he'd ever encountered who killed other beings for reasons other than for food or in self-defense.

Therefore, no matter what favors they might grant, bipeds were now and forever his enemies. This was a sad realization for Daniel.

To Lokat, Daniel argued that bipeds occasionally made mistakes and, therefore, the tribe could outwit them. Lokat disagreed, saying that since hunters swept through all the known seal colonies, for the tribe to flee from one place to another would only postpone the day of death. They must trust in Saul and hope that enough pups would be allowed to escape disaster.

Daniel did not yet know how the tribe would avoid the enemy next spring, but he was determined that it would. Anna and Meeyon were both pregnant, as were the other mature cows of the tribe. The new pups, he vowed, would have a greater chance to live. But how?

Cold weather arrived more rapidly than he had imagined possible. One day frost touched the morning dew; the next, icicles hung from kelva berry vines; on the third, clouds obscured the sun; and on the fourth day, a snowstorm lashed the inlet with violent winds. Daniel, Anna, Goshun, Meeyon, and her pup Filomena huddled in the lee of a boulder. When the storm cleared, a layer of white had softened the outlines of the inlet. A half-moon later, all three of the "southerners," as the cousins called them, were growing soft, brown, closely packed winter coats.

Winter deepened. Days became shorter, and often the sun could not be seen through the clouds, though the sky lightened during a half-tide to distinguish it from night. Nights themselves were longer; one could not sleep them through, and Daniel felt his system upset because he had to awaken and return to sleep in darkness. Ice blocked portions of the inlet, and on ocean trips to catch fish, Daniel noted that the shallows near some of the islands had frozen over. On one such trip he dove beneath a sheet of ice and was lucky that his old capacity for remaining on the bottom for long periods was still with him, because he lost his way and almost ran out of air before finding a hole to the surface. During another trip, he stayed atop the ice, but one of his diving companions among the cousins did not, and also was lost for some time. Then, in the distance, and through swirling snow, Daniel saw something that forced a lump to his throat: a great white-coated beast, erect on its hind legs. "Esmeralda!" he called, but the beast did not turn. Instead, it bent over a hole in the ice. The head of a seal appeared. Great claws and jaws fastened on it. A scream floated over the ice. Mists swirled, and, when they cleared, the beast and the cousin were gone.

After that, Daniel heeded the advice of Lokat, and went out on the ice only in company of several companions. In another half-moon, when much of the sea's surface was frozen over, it was possible to slip and slide the entire distance from the inlet to Bird's Neck. Lokat, Daniel, Parduk, and Vaz made the trip to the place where so many pups had died. Scavengers and storms had reduced the bodies to clean bones covered with snow. On the way back to the inlet, a blizzard swept down, and they could hardly see one another. When the males reached the inlet, they discovered that Parduk had vanished. She was never seen again.

During the winter moons, seals did not move about as they did in warmer weather, and needed less food. Absence of food, in turn, produced lethargy and a dreamlike state which fostered contemplation. The nights lasted so long that it was not reasonable to speak of "days." There was renewed, extensive ceremony honoring Beachmaster Saul, whose starry outline commanded the sky for most of the time the tribal members were awake. Even the occasional biped hunter, dressed in white fur, who came to overlook the tribe, seemed fascinated by the constellation of the great sea lion. Perhaps it was this odd interest on the part of the bipeds that, one night during verses asking for protection, pushed a thought into Daniel's brain: Beachmaster Saul must himself come down from his perch and defend the cousins from the biped hunters.

The snows blew harder, and the cousins dug lateral caves in drifts over water holes. In the course of spending a half-moon in a darkened snow cave, Daniel nurtured the thought of Saul coming down from the sky and figured out how this could be accomplished. It would be the greatest undertaking of Daniel's life, one that would utilize all he had learned through his journeys. In the name and in the manner of the Great Beachmaster, Daniel would gather the bulls around him and do battle with the sons of Kanonah.

He discussed the plan with Anna. Meeyon was agreeable and docile as a mate, but Anna's was the mind on which he depended. She said the idea was worthy, and set about to help. It was for the best, she told him, that Parduk was no longer among them, for she might have objected. Adherence to old patterns, Parduk's death had taught, was not the path of life but only of resignation to fate. Daniel and Anna agreed that the legend of Saul would only serve them if they made it do so.

Anna's first convert was Meeyon, who acknowledged Daniel's dominance and Anna's position as senior mate. With Meeyon's help, during the next half-moon, Anna stimulated a longing for the idea in the minds of the tribe's females, going from snow cave to snow cave, chatting amiably. All the females were pregnant, and none wished to lose a new pup.

When Daniel finally made the request of Lokat in front of everyone, the females spoke for it, the adolescent males who hoped to gain mates were with them, and even the youngest ones clamored to take part. Lokat was unable to refuse openly.

One morning Daniel heard a sound which the older cousins identified for him as the cracking and parting of blocks of ice. The time of the dark days passed. After a warm breeze had blown for three days in a row, Daniel said it was time to begin. Lokat nodded his head; however, it was clear to Daniel that neither the beachmaster of the seals nor their whistler, Vaz, gave the project their full approval.

Daniel was polite, but had no patience with their timidity. The great task was a certainty. All that remained was to force the image that he had in his mind to take shape upon the island. Calling to the bulls with a shout, he started over the cracking ice for Bird's Neck and his destiny.

16 · THE LAST ATTACK

*H*urrying out to Bird's Neck, Daniel and the bulls felt the ice breaking up beneath them; before reaching the island, they swam in open water. The warm breezes had brushed snow away from parts of the tundra; they smelled buds and the clear salt of the ocean. There was little sense of the violence that had taken place here nearly a cycle of moons ago.

Daniel set for the adolescents the task of assembling piles of whited bones. To the one-cycle bulls, Goshun among them, he awarded the chore of making mounds of shells. Alone, he gathered driftwood and pondered the best site for Beachmaster Saul. To put him atop the high rocks would mean having to haul materials too far; to erect him on the beach would leave him exposed to waves. Daniel chose a central spot on the belly of the bird, the site where the tribe usually massed together in kamarla. Saul would face both the beach and the rising sun.

For a quarter-moon they heaped materials and pushed them into a rough shape. Although the breadth and girth of the work seemed grand, Daniel judged the whole effect unsatisfactory. Where was the majestic, alert posture? The stern gaze that would greet the biped hunters as they came to kill?

When a sudden spring storm blew everything down,

Daniel was grateful for the chance to begin anew. This time he proceeded more slowly. It had to be correct, or it would not be good.

Using driftwood and muck brought up from the offshore bottom, Daniel fashioned a firm inner core to which outer materials could be affixed. He used all of his skill and many things that he recalled from the laboratory, such as constructing a series of bone platforms to support the massive head. Remembering how the creature on the sandbar had looked when stripped of flesh, he was able to mold the contours of the body into a lifelike shape. In an expedition to the bottom, Daniel harvested octopus sinews and had the seals pull them out in tug-tug games until they could be used to connect the scaffolds of bone. He also had a team search for three days to find large, iridescent abalone shells. For another quarter-moon Goshun did nothing but burnish these, but Daniel didn't tell him why. He was saving that detail for last.

Though the hunters would probably never see the nails on the flippers, he culled the husks from dozens of horseshoe crabs, with their projecting swords intact, to approximate this detail.

Bit by bit, the enormous thing took shape. Daniel's and the workers' sense of urgency was intensified by the gathering sweetness of the spring. Each evening they returned to the inlet, where the kelva berries were in bloom, where the cows burgeoned with what soon would be a new group of pups. Agwah, a late adolescent male, was hanging around Meeyon more than might be allowed by a jealous bull, but Daniel didn't mind, because Agwah acknowledged Daniel's own primacy and leadership in this as well as in all other matters.

One evening Daniel was unable to sleep. The task was half-complete, and he knew precisely what had to be done to finish it. His mind raced. Awake, he clambered to the top edge of the inlet closest to the bluff. Above him, the moon was full, and he heard the sound of a lone creature roaring at it. Earlier in the winter, he'd heard this low-pitched howl several times across the ice-blown landscape. The cousins told stories of polar bears dragging off careless pups. Daniel had once seen a white, craggy shape capture a seal—and yet he was drawn in the direction of the howl. By dint of tremendous effort, he scrambled up the boulders and reached the cliff.

A hundred lengths off, he saw the white polar bear—standing on hind paws, twice as large as a biped, and with talons and teeth ready to kill a seal or a sea lion.

"Don't come any closer," he barked, afraid in spite of himself.

"I won't eat you, Daniel."

"Esmeralda!"

They moved closer together. Daniel did not go and embrace the bear, however; he couldn't yet be sure if her words were a trap.

"You've lost weight," Daniel observed. "Harsh winter?"

"More so than usual. Are you enjoying your stay with the little ones?"

"In certain ways."

"You've become their leader."

"Not exactly. When my task is finished, I'll move on."

"I'm here to warn you. The biped hunters are coming soon."

They sat and talked. The dwelling place of the biped

hunters was not far from a forest in which Esmeralda's family had a home cave. During the winter, a biped had killed one of Esmeralda's cubs, and, in return, Esmeralda had killed two of the bipeds. Now, because of warmer weather, she would have to hide. But before disappearing she wanted to warn Daniel.

"We're not finished building yet," Daniel explained, and had to tell her about the great project to protect the cousins' beautiful white pups. Esmeralda's eyes glistened at the idea. She promised to send Daniel a signal when the biped hunters started for their floaters. She wasn't sure what that signal would be, but Daniel would recognize it.

"Thank you, Esme."

"One day, we'll hunt together!"

"That would be an honor."

As Daniel returned to the inlet under the baleful eye of the moon, Anna stirred.

"Did I hear you talking to yourself again?"

Daniel said nothing. He nuzzled her protruding belly and stretched out next to her for sleep.

~~~~

Late the next day, Daniel and the bulls looked up from their labors on the island to see the rest of the tribe approaching Bird's Neck. Daniel wished they had stayed on the mainland, but the cows had urgent need of the birthing ground. At the first sight of the half-completed icon, many of the females were afraid. Anna was astounded. So overcome was she that she could find nothing appropriate to say to Daniel; they had a brief, silent embrace.

Lokat was beside himself with anger. He called the statue

"an offense to Saul," and would have ordered the entire tribe to seek another place for the pups to be born—but Vaz, on examining the huge accumulation of bone, shell, wood, and other sea materials, immediately began the ceremony of the Singing, in as fervent a voice as ever he had raised to the sky. The remainder of the tribe followed Vaz's lead, and were rewarded by the sight of Saul's eye, winking in the twilight, and, soon after moonrise, the appearance of the entire constellation, glowing with what seemed an invigorated radiance.

Lokat was further annoyed the following day when the bulls fought one another for territories. Several of the full-grown males sought advice and protection from Daniel—from whom they had been used to taking orders in the building.

On the second day on the island, Anna gave birth. Daniel and Anna's second pup was a tan-coated female. Anna insisted that it be named Parduk, an idea that pleased Daniel.

The following day, Meeyon gave birth, and Daniel was relieved to note that the pup had a white coat. A pup of mixed parentage might have offended the touchy Lokat. Nevertheless, Daniel stood guard over both mates and their young.

Little Goshun chose that day to catch his first fish all by himself; he brought it to Anna and little Parduk to eat.

The adolescent bulls were drawn to the pleasures of fighting on the hauling ground, the mature bulls had territories to define—and so Daniel was left to work alone, day and night, to complete the icon. He stopped his labors only in the evening, to be present at the ceremony beseeching the Beachmaster in the Sky to spare the tribe from harm.

The moon shed her bright coat, passed through the cove of darkness, and put on a full new coat. One night, just before dawn, a faint doglike howl drifted over the waters, insistent and frightening. Was this Esmeralda's warning? Daniel could not be certain. All about the island, dozens of white pups lay sleeping. In the harsh light of the moon they were beautiful and helpless. If the attack were to come shortly, their protection would depend entirely upon his own work.

Determinedly Daniel climbed up the icon with one of Goshun's abalone shells in his mouth. He affixed the shell, shiny side out, to the left eye socket, then came down, got the other shell, and hauled himself up to insert it into the right orb. There were dozens of other details he wished to make perfect—the set of the hind flippers, the color of the mane—but time had run out. At dawn he lay on the promontory, exhausted, and waited for the floaters.

As the morning fog lifted, three floaters approached out of the rising sun. On the island the tribe awoke, saw the wooden biped things, and began singing. Some seals imagined blood, some rescue, but all raised moans to the sky. Their singing grew louder as the biped hunters, dark-faced and covered for warmth, shut off their whirlers and prepared to land on Bird's Neck's beach.

Facing the hunters was the mountainous icon of Beachmaster Saul. Higher than the top point of the island, as large as twenty sea lions, he sat on his haunches, flippers outstretched, shoulders erect and head alert, his multicolored eyes glowing with the power they reflected from the rising sun.

A giant sea lion was staring at the bipeds. Around the giant clustered an entire herd of seals. These were not the docile, harmless victims of thirteen moons ago; they were angry beasts under the protection of a creature not of this earth—so large, so lifelike, so unexpected—a giant sea lion descended from the stars.

For some moments, Daniel and the tribe watched as the floaters stood just offshore, waves smacking against their wooden sides. The bipeds looked and looked at Saul, and talked among themselves. Then the whirlers were started, the floaters were turned about and the bipeds headed back toward the mainland.

~~~

The cows cried. Lokat was silent. Vaz sang louder than ever. The furry white newborns, bewildered by all the emotion, sought their mothers for milk and comfort. As Daniel climbed down from the high rocks where he had watched the statue greet the bipeds, Anna rushed to embrace him. Soon the entire tribe surrounded him, and expressed love and gratitude. Daniel felt proud and thankful and very tired.

Next day, the hunters returned, this time in so many floaters that Daniel couldn't count them all. One of these pulled tentatively onto the beach, and Daniel became alarmed—perhaps the hunters thought to overwhelm the statue and the tribe with great numbers of bipeds. He was relieved to see that the bipeds simply carried salmon, crabs, and other food, and laid them between the outstretched flippers of the great statue.

Daniel did not want the tribe to eat any food from the

hands of the bipeds. Anna, who understood Daniel's mistrust, suggested that he was wrong. He relented, and they ate well.

It was this incident that finally convinced Lokat to go to Daniel and offer him his neck—in effect, ceding the leadership of the tribe. Lokat addressed him as "Beachmaster Daniel," and said he would follow him anywhere.

Daniel was amused at the idea that anyone could call him beachmaster, for he had never fought bulls or covered females so he could have such a title. It was this thought that allowed him to graciously refuse Lokat's offer, telling the old seal that he and his family would be traveling on as soon as the weather warmed sufficiently and the new pups were weaned and seaworthy. The region of ice was the home of the cousins, he said, not his own home.

"And where is your home, Daniel?"

The question amazed him, but now he had an answer for it. Remembering his youthful dream, he said, "Pacifica."

~~~~~

During the quarters of the next moon, many floaters came near the island—some, much larger than those of the hunters—to gaze at the statue, to bring offerings, and to point glass-and-metal devices at Daniel. Initially the humans' interest puzzled him. Why fix on him, in the midst of so many other animals? At last he realized that he was the animal on the island who most closely resembled the statue.

One day some bipeds who were lighter-skinned than the hunters, and who looked more like Karl and Fred, tried to

beach a floater on the island. Several other floaters full of
dark-skinned hunters prevented the first one from landing.
Biped voices were raised, and a stick was pointed that made
a loud noise. Blood came from one of the lighter-skinned
biped's arms, and all the floaters whirled away from the
beach.

After this, the tribe swam back to the inlet. Even though
Daniel had said that his family would now leave, they
stayed with the cousins through the glorious summer. The
kelva berries were particularly sweet, the flies seemed less
annoying than last cycle, and, of course, Daniel and Anna
did not want to leave before the naming ceremony for the
little cousins who had shed their white coats. Several were
named after Daniel, and he accepted the honor.

At that ceremony, in a new song suggested by Voola,
Vaz's one-eyed apprentice, the tribe celebrated the survival
of the pups. Everyone sang that the ancient Beachmaster
had come down from the sky to protect them, that Daniel
had done the bidding of the stars in making on the island
an image of Saul.

Daniel wondered if that were true, or if it was just a
conceit of the cousins. Had he merely been a tool of a
higher being when he fashioned the statue? Were his journeys and difficulties all part of a grand pattern that had
readied him for this particular task? Had he done the whole
thing himself, without the help or even the presence of
Beachmaster Saul? For that matter, had there ever been a
"real" Beachmaster Saul at all? Ever since his experience
in the sargasso with the crazed beast that resembled many
of the offspring of Saul—sea lion, dolphin, whale, bear,
and otter—he hadn't been sure whether there had ever

been an actual Beachmaster Saul or whether the legend was just a collection of old stories.

He and Anna decided at last that the truth was more complicated than any single explanation. Let the cousins believe that Saul had actually come down from the sky. Let others puzzle over whether Beachmaster Saul had been real or only legendary. What mattered was that Daniel believed in the legend and had created something from it that had scared the bipeds and had saved the pups.

Daniel also came to realize that, having made the statue, he was at last free of the memory of the dead pups that had haunted him for an entire cycle of moons.

On the morning of the first frost, Daniel and his extended family, which now included Anna, Goshun, Parduk, Meeyon, her lover Agwah, their daughter Filomena, and the just-named Oona, said their good-byes—swiftly, so no one would cry—and left the home cove of the cousins, swimming south.

17 · THE TRIBE

~~~~~~~~~~~~~~~~~~~~

The family of Daniel au Fond swam south at a leisurely pace, its progress defined by the capabilities of its youngest members. The group of eight was one of fortunate variety. The four adults hunted well together. Agwah and Meeyon knew more about the mosses and grasses of the small coastal islands than did the cove-reared Daniel and Anna; this contributed to the food supply. The one-cyclers and pups had companions for play.

Daniel insisted they island-hop, a strategy that had served him well in the past. In a tide pool one morning, he caught a glimpse of himself. He had aged. Now, at the height of his physical powers, he was slightly grizzled and bore plenty of scars. That day while on the ocean, he looked more carefully at Anna than he had in awhile. She, too, had aged, but he valued her more highly than he had in his adolescence. Her every glance showed understanding of his world. He and Anna had shared many experiences; often their communication had to do with these past events and feelings, recalled in words or expressions that had no meaning for the others. Anna tolerated, even encouraged, the presence of Meeyon in the tribe. Daniel told Anna that no perch mate would ever come between himself and her. They remembered together, he said; they had the gift of sharing more than the present moment, of building on the past to imagine a future.

The great task accomplished, Daniel enjoyed having more time to spend with the pups. Goshun was hard to manage, given to breaking away from the family for a romp alongside a large fish, now and then. Anna observed that he was, as yet, more silly otter than lion of the sea. Daniel wondered what old Popocatepetl would say about that! Parduk was equally as sassy as her older brother, and liked to hum songs before sleep. She, Filomena, and Oona, all immature females now, would need mates in a few cycles.

During their travels down the coast, the group saw seal and sea-lion colonies nestled in harbors that had many signs of biped civilization nearby. Daniel passed up all these colonies without visiting. However, individuals, or, sometimes, pairs of seals swam out to greet them. Twice Daniel was startled to hear the callers hail him by name. Evidently word had begun to spread, from family to family, tribe to tribe, about the great statue on Bird's Neck Island and the beachmaster who had built it. Naturally, some of the stories were distorted; one visitor was amazed to see that Daniel was not a giant.

One morning, a familiar shape loomed in their path—the white laboratory floater. No sooner had Daniel recognized it than he heard the noise of the opening in the bottom, and five seals swam out toward them. He gave the signal to Agwah and the others to remain on the alert, and not to let any of the red seals—or bipeds—near the pups. He and Anna swam forward to meet the oncoming red ones.

Banta and Blog, in the lead, were overjoyed to see him. Helen hung back for a moment, though not out of modesty, for it was apparent that the two seals whom Daniel didn't know, both males from her old tribe, deferred to her, as did Banta and Blog. Daniel introduced Anna, and Banta told them that Fred and the entire floater had recently gone to the north to see the great statue on Bird's Neck Island, and that the local seals had told them that Daniel had made it appear on the island by magic.

None of the five southern, earless seals wore necklaces or metal-whisker devices in their shoulders. "What happened to the signal senders?" Daniel asked. "And the necklaces? Where's Sigmund?"

Helen came forward to answer. They swam at the surface, two dozen lengths from the floater. As they spoke, Daniel watched a small floater being lowered over the side of the larger one. It had no whirler, but a biped used several long sticks to propel it in Daniel's direction.

Helen said that after Daniel's escape Fred had screamed and stomped about the floater until the metal-whisker devices were removed from all the animals. Then he'd trained and trained the seals until they knew enough to come back to him or to the floater when summoned—and the necklaces also had been thrown away. As for Sigmund, well, he was still on the floater, though he never spoke to the seals.

The small biped floater pushed by the two sticks drew closer, and Daniel recognized Fred. Another creature stuck its head up from beneath the wood. It was Sigmund. Fred gazed at Daniel from behind his glasses and made the hand signal of greeting; Sigmund just stared at him. Daniel tossed his head to acknowledge their presence, but would not swim within petting distance.

The trainer leaned over the side of the small floater, and seemed to want very much to scratch Daniel in back of the ears. Daniel wished Fred no harm, and he remembered actually liking being scratched by Fred in the laboratory. He thought about allowing Fred to do it, but did not. One good biped couldn't make up for an enemy race of bloodthirsty hunters who killed pups. Besides, Daniel thought, he was trying to emulate Saul's ways and be a beachmaster in earnest, now, and he would have to deny himself some small pleasures in order to maintain a clear mind.

"Daniel," Sigmund said abruptly, "you're famous now. How did you make that statue?"

"There were many of us involved. Tell me—should we overturn Fred's floater and rescue you?"

"I can't swim," Sigmund replied.

"You could ride on my back. We've got a legend about land creatures doing something like that, my friend."

Sigmund was thoughtful for a moment. "It might be exciting, if difficult. But not now, Daniel."

"Why not?"

"I've begun communicating with the bipeds much more directly," he said. He made a few sounds with his mouth that were remarkably bipedlike. Fred, in the small floater, seemed startled to hear them. "As soon as I complete that task, I'll be ready."

"Come now. Freedom doesn't wait."

"Soon," said the orange one.

Banta swam up to Daniel, looked him in the eye, and said, "Ah'll go with you."

"Me, too," Blog echoed.

"You boys'll stay right heah with me," Helen shouted, alarmed.

Daniel laughed and headed straight for the bottom. There, he gave the signal for the family to thrust out to sea at full speed. The ten of them were more than a match for Helen. Above, Fred banged the sides of the floater in frustration. Helen followed for a thousand lengths, then turned back with the other two males. In the far distance, Daniel saw Fred and Sigmund being hauled up in their small floater to the mother one.

The traveling group of ten was of three different tribes: Daniel, Anna, Goshun, and Parduk of the brown sea lions; Meeyon, Agwah, and their brood of dappled seals; and the red-brown southern seals Banta and Blog.

~~~~

Two nights later the group reached Small Crab Island. It had hardly enough perches for all. Daniel announced that they would shortly go to his and Anna's old home cove, and warned that this would be the most dangerous territory they had yet encountered. He described the warm waters, the food and wafers from the bipeds; his followers pledged not to partake of any of the cove's offerings.

In the morning, after a half-tide of swimming, the family reached the outer limits of the cove. As of old, no barrier but the shift in water temperature prevented entrance or exit. Daniel recognized various sites from his youth—the cleft Singing Stones, the Whistler's Shelf, Elbow Overhang; this time he was not overwhelmed by the memories associated with these spots. Anna seemed more nervous than he did at being here.

By cove standards it was still early in the day, and the sea lions lay out on the rocks, sleeping or taking the sun. There were Hagis and Achitopel, his old brothers, and the now-mature females Zelda and Marlena, Anna's old sisters. The two mothers, Blossom and Esther. Of the others, Anna recognized more individuals than Daniel did. She whispered that although the males and females were older, they were all still handsome, displaying the special sheen of those who are well-fed and well-exercised but have no cares or real tasks. Daniel and Anna were reminded of the shorter, more compact cousins, whose worn countenances possessed so much more character than the individuals in this cove.

"Whut a sway-ull place," Banta observed.

"Yes, and the cows you've been eyeing are quite beautiful. Just remember: We're not staying long, and we're not to eat any of their food."

"Uh-huh. Ah also ought to tail you thet Fred and the floater ah jes' outside of heah."

"Thank you. Let me know if they make any moves."

To Daniel, the cove seemed to have been altered in subtle but important ways: more perches, more smooth rocks on which to climb up. It had never previously been possible to dive off Elbow Overhang, because the bottom had been too shallow; now, that part of the cove had been deepened so that bipeds watching from the escarpment could have the pleasure of seeing the animals make spectacular dives from the high rocks into the water.

Blog came by and took him to what Daniel noted was another changed feature: Below the waterline, on the northern arm and near the glass window, there were rows of sticks, egg-shapes, and pattern glasses. Daniel wondered if the cove had become a laboratory.

"Want to see how the game works, strangers?" Zelda, one of the females of Daniel's birth cohort, had swum down, and immediately began to operate the sticks. In the midst of the pattern glass, the outline of a shark could be seen, undulating as if it were coming toward the watching animals. Colored lights pulsed and changed in the glass. Zelda pushed on a clamshell device, and the shark-shadow exploded. She grinned, then gave her full attention to the game. More shadowy "enemies" came into view in the glass. When Daniel asked her a question, she was too absorbed with the game to hear him. Other cove dwellers swam down and played with the remaining pattern glasses in a similar manner.

Daniel returned to the surface, and there was Tashkent. The old leader's eyes followed Daniel's little family as they moved about the cove. He was now more white-furred, bulky, and seemed tired. As the day wore on it became painfully obvious to Daniel that Tashkent was no longer the dominant bull of the tribe.

The leadership had passed to Hagis and Achitopel, but had not been settled between them. The jokester and the food lover followed each other about, roaring threats and making occasional lunges which always seemed to miss the mark. However, when any other bull swam by, both Hagis and Achitopel would turn on him and make sure the third one did not capture a perch or approach any of the females they currently fancied. Together they pushed Agwah away from Marlena.

The dappled cousin wished to make a run at them, one at a time, but thought he should check first with Daniel. "They not beachmasters," Agwah said. "They like make noise but not fight."

"You're right about that. But it means they're not real threats, either. Get what you want by craft, not direct challenge."

"Aha."

Agwah swam to his task, and Daniel was certain he'd easily outwit Hagis and Achitopel. As for himself, he wished only that his old brothers would say hello, but knew they didn't even recognize him.

Eventually, it was the little ones who broke through the cove's indifference. The females there hadn't seen pups in many a cycle. Curiosity acted as a stimulus to maternal feelings, and soon Zelda, Marlena, and especially the two older cows, Blossom and Esther, were having a good time with the pups and one-cyclers. Daniel became concerned when Esther offered little Goshun a snack, but was proud as his son politely refused the food and said he was able to trap his own. It was also the pups who finally roused Tashkent the Terrible—how inappropriate the name now sounded! His great bulk cresting waves in front of him, the former leader swam slowly over to the gathered crowd of seals and sea lions.

"And who might these little ones be, Daniel?"

"You know who I am!"

"I had forgotten much, but not that, my son."

"Am I truly your son, Tashkent?"

"With so many offspring, one can't be sure—but you must be."

"Then these 'must be' your grandpups."

The old bull was pleased, and joined the observers of the pups. In time he allowed little Goshun to make a mock charge at him, and let the sassy Parduk chew on his whiskers.

~~~~

Tashkent told Daniel that after the great battle, he had extracted himself from the cleft in the Stones, but was very weak. For many days he could swallow no food or wafers, and, while regaining his strength, he also discovered that certain memories were returning to him. Once having recovered his health, he no longer cared to maintain dominance in the cove, and had retired without a fight. In the final reckoning, no bull had been able to wrest the leadership from him; he had just given it up. Now Tashkent was content to bask in the sun, eat the food, but not the wafers, which, he said, clouded his mind. He'd chat with the older cows and watch the bipeds on the cliff—who were, he snorted, almost as foolish in their ways as Hagis and Achitopel.

"There are questions I've longed to ask you," Daniel said.

"About the typhoon and its aftermath?"

"How did you—?"

"Because I think about them all the time, and wonder, even now, if I made the right choice."

They spent the rest of the day side by side on two adjoining ledges, and Tashkent told Daniel what had ensued in the days just after the great typhoon.

As Daniel had guessed, Goshun had then been the dominant bull and Tashkent the newly matured challenger for the leadership. The younger bull had impregnated many of the cows, and most of them were killed during the typhoon. For the first few days after the tragedy, when the bipeds brought the tribe to this cove, the time had been spent in recuperating and in mourning the dead and the lost. Then had come the crisis. Citing the old tale of the irreconcilable split between Beachmaster Saul and the biped Kanonah, Goshun had argued that the tribe must immediately leave the cove and have nothing further to do with the bipeds. He admitted that the tribe was under strength, with few bulls to provide protection, and that pups and one-cyclers would probably not survive long on the open seas; in fact, he embraced the possibility that the tribe itself could be decimated. Better this death, Goshun had argued, than existence at the mercy of the bipeds.

Tashkent knew all too well that living in a cove, accepting the food and protection of the bipeds, was no life for a true sea lion. But he was not ready to go to his own death, and certainly was not inclined to lead the tribe into complete oblivion. Far better, he had shouted at Goshun, to accept shelter from the hated bipeds at the moment and wait until the tribe had regained its strength to once again take to the open sea.

Goshun and Tashkent had fought then, for days and nights on end; their fight was not only for physical mastery but for the direction the tribe would take. Eventually Tashkent's youth had prevailed. Goshun had been given the Whistler's Shelf, a position of veneration and honor. However, over the ensuing cycles, as the tribe had settled into the cove life, something had happened. Memories of the past had vanished, and with them went the age-old mistrust of bipeds. Now, five cycles later, most of the sea lions praised the bipeds, even loved them for their hand-outs and the protected life they made possible.

Perhaps only he, Tashkent believed, still remembered that the sea lions had made a bargain with the bipeds—had given up freedom for safety. As waves slowly but contin-uously erode a cliff, so the tribe's courage in maintaining a danger-filled life had been leached away by the bipeds' steady provision of food, shelter, and warmth. Time pass-ing had added certainty to the original decision. No pups appeared to augment the tribe, and there seemed no reason to leave what had become a comfortable home. Through many cycles Tashkent had not questioned his original decision. Then Goshun died, Daniel had bested him in a fight, he had stopped eating the wafers, and had again begun to think. The sad thing was, Tashkent said, that the Whistler had gone into the sun with his differ-ences with Tashkent unresolved. In Tashkent's view, Go-shun had never forgiven Tashkent for his decision.

"No wonder Goshun thought you weren't a 'real' beachmaster."

"Perhaps it's true. Maybe I did fail the tribe in believing what I was doing was for the good of everyone."

"You were—you are—a real beachmaster," Daniel said with conviction. "On this point, Goshun was . . . perhaps too angry to be completely right."

"In many ways, I never knew him."

Daniel nodded but did not speak. Tashkent, he vowed, would not go to his own death without a son who loved him.

"You know, Daniel, you also are a real beachmaster."

"How is that?"

"Because you have been doing things that help others beyond yourself and claiming nothing in return but respect."

Daniel swallowed hard. Yes, he thought, that was true—and so simple. Why hadn't it occurred to him before? And why hadn't Goshun mentioned it to him? Maybe each "true" beachmaster had to discover it for himself. Now even Tashkent knew it. Indeed, the old tyrant had changed.

"You know," the old bull said, "I could have killed you that day on Bright Corner."

"But you didn't. And I didn't finish you either. Serves us both right." Daniel laughed and Tashkent joined him. Their conversation had been a quiet one, and the sea lions around them couldn't figure out why the bulls were laughing so loudly or acting so friendly.

Anna swam up and whispered something in Daniel's ear; he in turn asked Tashkent if they could continue the conversation later. Tashkent smiled. The older females were spoiling the pups, Zelda and Marlena were primping for Banta and Blog, and, below, Meeyon and Agwah were having a go at the pattern glass—so Daniel and Anna could slip away.

They quickly hopped up the ledges toward Grunting Cave, wanting to see if the place was still wondrous. As they were getting cozy in the cave, faint colored lights began to glow, and the darkness yielded to dimness. The experience was disappointing.

When they emerged, the Singing had begun. Little Goshun rested in the flippers of Tashkent. Meeyon and the rest of the family sat on the outer ledges, while Esther and Blossom led the herd. The departing red-gold rays of the sun and the rhythmic humming of the stones were enchanting. Though Daniel hadn't voiced the words aloud in some moons, he sang them quietly to himself with great pleasure. However, when Esther and Blossom intoned the verse that substituted thanks to the bipeds for their rescue for the verse that honored Beachmaster Saul, Daniel sang out, loud and clear:

"Deep, the realm of Beachmaster Saul,
Great-great-grandfather of us all.
Dark, Pacifica's storied walls,
Yet still, the monarch sounds his call:"

And he was surprised when Tashkent's booming voice joined him in singing:

" 'Come, lions that dwell in the sea,
We travel far in mystery!' "

There were no comments from the cove sea lions, but Daniel knew from glances he received that other tribal members were unhappy at the changes he and Tashkent had sung. Not so Little Goshun. He asked Daniel about the Singing.

"The sea lion whom you were named for taught it to me."

"Can I learn it?"

"Maybe Grandpa Tashkent will teach you," he whispered. "But not right now."

Food and wafers were being delivered to the colony. Daniel ordered his family not to eat anything from the hands of the bipeds; should anyone be hungry, he personally would bring them something choice from outside the cove walls. Daniel felt that he was stifling possible enjoyment by this order, but knew he must protect his family from the subtle attractions of the cove. He did, however, encourage Blog and Banta to consummate their pursuits of Zelda and Marlena. The southern males needed mates, and the family needed more females to increase its numbers. He suggested to Banta and Blog that they prevent Zelda and Marlena from eating wafers this night if they could, so their minds would be clearer in the morning.

Out of the corner of his eye, Daniel saw Karl, the biped, but tried to show no sign that he'd seen. The bipeds wouldn't come after the sea lions at night, but the family ought to leave at first light. He told Tashkent his plan.

"You know, Daniel, when I started to think that I'd made a bad bargain with our enemies, one that hurt the tribe, I began also to mull over the story of Kanonah and Saul. Having myself lived under the bipeds for many cycles, it's clear to me that we have missed something in the legend."

"What?"

"Don't get so agitated, Daniel. Everyone forgets things, and this part of the legend probably didn't sit comfortably with Goshun. It often happens that facts that don't fit into our view of the world are thrown away or hidden by our minds."

"Out with it, Tashkent!"

"I don't remember it precisely, but there was a fragment that said that Kanonah, even more than Saul, suffered when he took Selchie away from the sea lions and broke the bargain he had made."

"But Kanonah broke the bargain—why would he suffer?"

"Kanonah suffered—as I do—because he knew that he had done a great wrong, and that there was no way to set it right."

Daniel was silent for a few moments, then spoke quietly. "Are we to pity the bipeds, and not hate them?"

"Perhaps we must do both."

"I'm not ready to forgive them yet. Their bad deeds grow daily in number and subtlety."

"Sleep on it," the old bull said.

During the night, the team of Hagis and Achitopel—emboldened by the wafers—tried to drag Meeyon away from the circle of perches that Daniel and the family occupied. Agwah took a ferocious nip out of the extra-large hindquarters of Achitopel the food lover, and the "leaders" retreated. No other incidents marred the dark tides. It did not escape Daniel's notice that Banta and Blog did not sleep with the family group.

Morning came. A cycle ago, when he and Anna had been about to leave, they'd railed bitterly against the conditions here and the stupidity of the sea lions in accepting gifts from the bipeds. Daniel knew now, from his discussions with Tashkent, that they'd changed no minds. This time, Daniel spoke loudly to the sea lions in the cove, but accused no one, least of all Tashkent, who watched silently from a perch above Elbow Overhang. He stated simply that he was forming a new family, and that all were welcome in it. He asked for sea lions to join him, to harken to the old monarch's call, to "travel far in mystery."

On the escarpment, and from openings hidden in the cove's arms—which, despite a careful search, Daniel had not noticed—bipeds in sea-lion coverings stepped or slid into the water.

"Come on," Daniel barked. "All that would journey with Daniel au Fond, we leave now!" Only Zelda and Marlena moved with the family, swimming fearfully next to Blog and Banta, whose soft voices urged them on. There were almost as many bipeds swimming through the cove as there were members of the new family. And, just beyond the entrance, Daniel could see the laboratory floater. Bipeds might trap them from both sides! He needed all the strength he could muster.

"Tashkent!" he screamed. "Come with us."

"Too late, Daniel. I've made my perch, now I'll lie on it."

"You haven't forgotten how to swim!"

"I'm too old. I'd only slow you down."

"You're no slower than the pups. They need you as much as I do. It's never too late to be free!"

With a roar and a great crash, the old bull dove down from Elbow Overhang, making a great wave that threw two of the swimming bipeds off course. He aimed at two more; at his approach, they split off and swam aside, letting him through. He became the final link in the family that Daniel was leading out to the edge of the cold water.

The floater was closing in on the mouth of the cove. Daniel could see Fred the trainer and Sigmund the orangutan atop the floater, setting fire to some red-colored sticks.

"To the bottom," Daniel yelled, almost without thinking. It had always been his refuge, and must save him now.

As the huge side of the floater loomed before them, the column of seals and sea lions did as Daniel ordered—and passed easily underneath the floater and away on the open-water side, heading west. Daniel moved and let the others by him, then turned to be ready to fight the bipeds if he had to.

At just this moment on the cove side of the floater, in the water, there were blinding flashes of light as well as deafening explosions. Whatever the red sticks were that Fred and Sigmund had thrown at the bipeds, their effects were stunning. The swimming bipeds in sea-lion coverings floated up to the surface. Some held their heads. Others ripped the glass from their faces, revealing bloodied noses.

Daniel himself was momentarily blown back by the red sticks that exploded, but he saw his family reach the surface a hundred lengths away, and swim west, toward Small Crab Island.

Fred spotted him, and he saw the old trainer. Their eyes locked. Fred made the old hand signal that said "go," and pointed to the horizon. Daniel blinked, barked a farewell to him, and sped off to rejoin his family.

"Fred helped us," Daniel said when he caught up to Tashkent and the family. "The biped actually assisted us in getting away from the others of his race."

"That makes it harder to hate all bipeds," Tashkent answered. Daniel had to agree.

The big old bull was puffing heavily from the unusual exertion of open-ocean swimming, so Daniel ordered everyone to slow down a bit. Little by little, they realigned themselves into a comfortable yet alert traveling column. He took the lead, followed by Anna; the mature males were at the flanks, protecting the secondary females and offspring in the center; Tashkent brought up the rear. Daniel noted that they were thirteen, a fitting number for the inheritors of the tradition of Beachmaster Saul.

By evening, they reached Small Crab Island for a much-needed rest.

As the new tribe sat on the craggy rocks of the small island that night, underneath the stars, Tashkent formally asked Daniel to accept the title of beachmaster and to advise them of their future direction. Daniel accepted the leadership, and said that the new tribe would set out to recapture the days of glory that had always been associated with the time of Beachmaster Saul. Tashkent would be the tribe's Whistler and would teach them as much about the old times as he could. But there was more to the legend of Saul than even the Whistler knew, and it would be the tribe's task to discover and learn everything about it. Also, new members had to be found—a task which was intertwined with the first, because knowledge about the ancient days lay in the minds of the scattered descendant tribes of Beachmaster Saul. They would visit these tribes, try to learn from them, and, eventually, having adequate knowledge, they would search for the ancient home cove of Pacifica. If fulfilling these tasks meant roaming the world, that was what they would do.

Next morning just after dawn, the small tribe of seals and sea lions under the leadership of Beachmaster Daniel au Fond set out on the open ocean in search of a legend.